T0098985

SAND TRAP

SAND TRAP

INTERNATIONAL TREACHERY,
NEFARIOUS PLOTS,
& PERSONAL AWAKENINGS

J. E. DANIELS

Carpenter's Son Publishing

Sand Trap
International Treachery, Nefarious Plots, & Personal Awakenings

©2023 J.E. Daniels

All rights reserved. No part of this book may be reproduced or transmitted in any form or by any means, electronic or mechanical, including photocopying, recording, or by any information storage and retrieval system, without permission in writing from the copyright owner.

The Authorized (King James) Version of the Bible ('the KJV'), the rights in which are vested in the Crown in the United Kingdom, is reproduced here by permission of the Crown's patentee, Cambridge University Press.

Published by Carpenter's Son Publishing, Franklin, Tennessee

Edited by Anne Tatlock

Cover and Interior Design by Suzanne Lawing

Printed in the United States of America

978-1-954437-87-6

This is a fictional story. It does not portray or describe any literal individual, group, organization, or ocurrence. The likeness of any historical/famous figures has been used fictitiously; the author does not speak for or represent these people. All opinions expressed in this book are the author's or fictional.

This book is dedicated

to everyone

who TREASURES our

GOD-GIVEN FREEDOMS!

CONTENTS

Chapter One

EVIL WITH A SMILE

Beads of sweat collected on Drockden Sorrell's eyebrows as he ran for his life. They splashed to his cheeks. His thirty-nine-year-old body battled for breath with all its might. Sweat drenched his shirt. Two angry assailants were close behind, running down the back streets of Washington, DC.

Drockden pulled away and cut through the alley as he raced with all his strength. He struggled down the sidewalk of the parallel street. Then he spotted a tattered 1996 Dodge Neon parked across the street. As a car enthusiast, he knew this could be useful.

Rapidly, Drockden crossed the street and raced to the car. Taking a knife with a small pick from his pocket, he unlocked the car door. He crawled in the back, pulled down the top of the back seat with the strap, and climbed into the trunk. Quietly, he pulled the fold-down seat top back into place.

Exhausted, Drockden remained still on his back and held the seat in place with his hand and the strap. He tried to be motionless and totally silent. He took long, slow breaths as sweat poured from his face and dripped to the trunk floor. The assailants' feet pounded loudly on the sidewalk as they drew nearer. His apprehension increased as he listened to their approaching footsteps, then somewhat lessened as they passed by.

Drockden waited until he felt it was safe, then slowly and carefully exited the automobile. Immediately, he darted back into the alley and retreated the way he had come. He heard the assailants' feet running in the distance, and someone screamed, "FIND HIM."

Panting, Drockden fought exhaustion as he ran. He pushed forcefully up the hill, passing several buildings, and dashed down the next street. He rested against a building and leaned his head back against the bricks. He groaned and sighed. "Uhhh!"

Silently, Drockden scanned every direction and again ran. Pain caused him to almost tumble. He stopped and rubbed his aching right calf. Desperate, he pressed forward. Finally, he saw his hotel.

Drockden ran up the steps. He tripped and almost faltered but regained his balance. He reached the archway entrance, looked around, and entered the hotel lobby. Drockden rushed through the hotel atrium to the elevator and pressed the button for the second floor. He was breathing a bit slower now. Exiting the elevator, he walked down the hallway to his room.

Opening the door, Drockden was stunned to find Sam seated in a chair. Sam was in his usual exquisite suit, with his eight-hundred-dollar haircut and manicured nails. Sam looked up and viciously smiled, with all his old-man wrinkles glaring.

"So, it's the famous Drockden Sorrell once again. Loved by all," Sam said.

Drockden's surprise quickly turned to trepidation.

Sam continued. "That'll be handy. 'You can run, but you can't hide.' Not even registered under a fake name."

"I'll never help you. Never!" Drockden shouted.

A massive, muscular man walked up behind Drockden.

"Sure, you will," Sam replied. "Meet Harry. Helping us or joining us will be easier than the alternatives. Especially for your family members. How do you think we control politicians, judges, attorneys general, and anybody else we need? Well, those who can't just be bought."

Drockden looked at Harry and tried to get away. Harry grabbed him with one of his colossal hands. Drockden struggled, but Harry promptly forced him back into the room. Harry closed the door and guarded it. Drockden glared at Sam.

"Look, I'm sorry your client's heart's broken, but this is crazy," Drockden said. "You can't make me help you. And you're going to get caught."

"That's where you're wrong. Twice. It's easier than you think. And soon, you'll be begging to help us," Sam predicted.

Drockden snarled at Sam. "Uh. Let me think. It's freezing in here." Drockden walked toward the thermostat.

"Don't change that temperature. You're just all sweaty and not in a suit," Sam said sternly.

Drockden pulled the bedspread off the bed and wrapped it around himself. He paced from one side of the room to the other.

"What are we talking about exactly? And how long will it take?" Drockden asked.

Sam was excited. "That's more like it. I'd—"

Drockden ran and jumped through the window, using the bedspread for protection. Harry rushed to the window.

"GET HIM," Sam shouted.

"The building's surrounded," Harry grinned. "They'll get him."

Harry lifted a two-way radio from his belt and called his henchmen. Looking out of the broken window, he saw the bedspread crumpled on the grass, surrounded by shards of glass. The beautifully landscaped area of the hotel was adjacent to an incredible park. Three ruffians in suits were chasing Drockden, but he had a lead.

Chapter Two

HEROES BRIGHTEN THE DAY

TEN MONTHS LATER:
US Temporary Military Group in Riyadh, Saudi Arabia.

Marines were standing at attention in the bright, hot desert sun. Lt. Colonel Grayson was forty years old and quite handsome, with dark brown hair, blue-gray eyes, a commanding six-foot-one-inch stature, and excellent posture.

Grayson inspected each soldier. A jeep arrived with Mark Hillsborough and Drockden Sorrell. Grayson smiled and walked to meet them. Mark and Drockden were laughing as they exited the jeep. Reaching Lt. Colonel Grayson, the driver saluted.

"Lt. Colonel Grayson, sir. Reporters Mark Hillsborough and Drockden Sorrell delivered as instructed, sir," the driver reported.

Grayson returned the salute, radiating masculinity and confidence.

"At ease, son." Grayson smiled and shook hands with Mark and Drockden. "Glad you could come. I hope your trip was good."

Grayson eagerly watched and listened to Drockden.

"The flight was rough and the turbulence terrible—what a day. And the stewardesses were all dog ugly," Drockden said.

Grayson's smile slowly lessened, and he looked very perplexed.

***

The morning turned to noon. Grand dunes rose in the distance, while waves of heat shimmered over the road. A bus came into view, cutting through the sandy desert that stretched as far as you could see in each direction. Carol Page, a pretty thirty-six-year-old critical care nurse, determinedly ran to catch the bus. Thirty-two-year-old Sandy Morrison, also a critical care nurse, tried frantically to keep up.

They were both in reasonably good physical shape, but the heat was draining. Carol and Sandy wore the used-to-be mandatory head and hair coverings for women, the hijab. They had agreed to wear it to get their jobs here coming from the US to work. It made them even hotter. Although the Crown Prince lightened various rules in the last five or six years, many Saudi families still required a head covering. The long abaya robe covering the arms and body was a stifling material and was often black, making the women even hotter. However, some of those rules were currently changing, as well.

Carol and Sandy did not have to wear an abaya, just the hijab. However, they complied with wearing modest, loose-fitting long dresses or skirts and tops that covered their arms, chest, and shoulders to be sure they were reserved enough.

Just to be on the safe side, hiring companies outside of Saudi Arabia often still require the employees to follow the old traditions. The companies wanted no problems with any current ruler or the Saudi population. Brown-haired Carol and bleached-blonde Sandy looked forward to shaking their heads and letting their hair flow after they got these hot coverings off back home on the compound. Many workers from lots of other countries lived there.

"Sandy, hurry up. They won't wait," Carol yelled.

"I'm coming," Sandy responded.

The two western women ran harder and arrived at the bus stop just in time. They breathlessly boarded the bus and paid their fares using their SAPTCO's rechargeable smart cards. It was much cheaper using the card than paying for single bus rides. Plus, they could recharge the card at one of the ticket vending machines using the SAPTCO app, or even with the bus driver. It was easy and convenient.

Carol and Sandy moved toward the back of the bus and sat down. It felt good to rest after running in the heat.

"Ah, air conditioning," Carol said, relishing the cool.

"We made it. I heard that Chris Pratt and Scarlett Johansson are going to Khobar. He's so cute." Sandy sighed with a dreamy look.

"And so married," Carol replied.

"Well, he's still cute, and I don't break the hands-off rule by just looking," Sandy said and nodded firmly.

The bus hit a bump and jostled everyone. Carol grabbed the bar, and Sandy held onto the seat.

"I bet none of this is true. We'll end up on another one of your wild goose chases," Carol smirked.

"Lighten up, Carol. You've been in this desert too long. We've got three days off work; let's have some fun. It's an adventure," Sandy insisted.

"Being hot and sweaty is more torture than adventure. I hate wearing these long dresses. I feel like we're shopping in the Stone Age," Carol scowled. "At least we don't have to wear a niqab covering all of our face, except for our eyes."

"Hush! You're going to get us in trouble. Talk about something else. Look, there's a camel." Sandy pointed, changing the subject.

"Oh, dear." Carol rolled her eyes. "How many celebrities are supposed to be coming to this royal wedding bash?"

"Lots, and it'll go on for days. But it's very secretive. The reporters can't even find out stuff," Sandy explained.

The bustling market came into view. "Wow. There are tons of people here today," Sandy observed.

Carol looked at Sandy. "There have always been massive amounts of people here every time we've come. Today's no different. Where have you been?"

"It just seems like more today," Sandy said. "Maybe because I will be able to shop for the first time. I am not just running in to pick up one thing. I know you've been here many times, but this is my first full adventure here."

The bus stopped with a jolt. "We made it," Sandy said, and they exited the bus.

Sandy was so excited she hardly knew which way to go first. They surveyed the market, called a souk, and sometimes found even amid high-rise buildings or shopping malls. Sandy went left down the first street. Then some colorful scarves caught her eye, and she turned right onto another road. Carol chuckled as she watched Sandy so full of joy.

Every direction had rows of tables that lined both sides of the streets. One table had handbags, one jewelry, another dresses, fabrics, produce, and more. A woman walked by wearing lots of large bracelets on her arms.

"I want to get a gold bracelet. I've heard they're pretty cheap here," Sandy admitted.

"They are," Carol agreed.

"But I don't want a big one. All that gold looks heavy and hot," Sandy remarked, perusing the goods.

More women walked by wearing excessive jewelry. Sandy scanned each bracelet.

"Yeah, try taking blood pressure with those. But have a little understanding; these women need that jewelry," Carol explained.

"Why?" Sandy questioned.

"Women were not allowed to own property for centuries. That's changed or is changing, but not everyone is certain it won't revert to the old custom. Remember?" Carol raised her brows at Sandy.

"Oh, yeah. But can't the ladies leave some of it in a jewelry box at home?" Sandy suggested.

"I'm sure they do. But if their husband decides to get rid of them, sometimes what they have on is what they get. It's a type of safety net," Carol explained with a frown.

"Shush! You'll get us arrested," Sandy warned with genuine concern.

A group of Arab men walked by them. Sandy discretely watched as Carol shook her head.

"But some of these Arab guys are cute," Sandy admitted.

"Get a grip. I know it's hard to acclimate to these restrictive social norms. The Saudis do not date, and they do not allow dating! I get that you are missing the western way of life, but, you know, nobody here dates. We were warned multiple times. It is not allowed, like many other things—"

Suddenly, there were excessive crowd noises and yelling as people rushed down to the next street.

"What is it?" Sandy asked.

"I don't know. Let's find out," Carol answered and followed the crowd down the street.

When they reached the corner, they spotted two western women attired in dresses that were far too short, showing their legs way above their knees. Some of the locals were throwing small rocks at the women's uncovered legs. The crowd cheered and shouted approval, encouraging the attackers to continue.

"What are they doing?" Sandy asked.

"They used to have the Mutaween, the religious police I warned you about, who would whip your ankles and legs if they weren't covered. Or poke you with a cane," Carol whispered. "But they got rid of that practice, although some locals continue the tradition in their own way. Those women should have known better than to dress like that here!"

"Should we try to help them?" Sandy asked with concern and trepidation.

Just then, Lt. Colonel Grayson, in civilian clothes, walked up behind Carol and Sandy. Everyone kept focused on the two women having their naked legs attacked.

"Miss, please take very small, slow steps down this side street," Grayson said, pointing to the road.

Carol turned around. "Excuse me. Not all females are submissive—"

"Lady, shut up. I don't care what you are. I'm simply trying to help you avoid a scene like the one you're observing," Grayson responded firmly.

"We're covered sufficiently and should have no problems," Carol replied emphatically.

"Tell that to your friend's skirt that has come unbuttoned up to her upper thigh. I saw the flesh-flashing from across the road," Grayson declared.

Sandy's eyes widened. She grabbed Carol's arm. They silently looked at each other with sheer panic and then at Grayson. The three of them moved cautiously down the street, not wanting to draw any attention toward themselves. Grayson guided the women into an alley passageway.

"Bend as little as possible and button your skirt," Grayson instructed. He motioned to Carol. "You stand on that side so we can create a barrier."

Carol moved as directed. Sandy meanwhile discovered that the buttonholes of her skirt were slightly too big, allowing the buttons to slip through and leave her leg exposed. She carefully and gently buttoned her skirt as quickly as possible without making any drastic movements. It helped that everyone else was still watching the other two women.

Grayson, on the other hand, was intently watching someone else in the distance. As she finished buttoning her skirt, Sandy discreetly looked at Grayson's left hand and noted with satisfaction that his ring finger was bare. She also could not help noticing her rescuer's handsome good looks and charm.

"Thank you so much. That was a close call," Carol admitted.

"You said we were safe!" Sandy fussed. "I could have huge welts all over my legs from rocks or be rotting to death somewhere from being stoned."

Carol patted her arm. "It's okay. Don't be so dramatic. Problem solved."

Sandy clutched her chest and sighed. Relieved, she touched Grayson's arm. "Thank you so—"

Carol quickly jerked Sandy's arm away from Grayson.

"No touching. You can't touch him. You're not married. You'll both get arrested, and you'll get fired," Carol warned emphatically.

"I forgot," Sandy admitted with a petrified look.

Grayson was focused on someone in the distance still. "Ladies, I think you're fine now. Good luck." He walked away quickly.

"Hey, what's your name?" Sandy called. Grayson was preoccupied, and she received no reply.

"That's it, bring more attention to us," Carol scolded. "We're lucky we didn't get in trouble. That would put both our jobs in major jeopardy. Plus, we'd have to pay back all our advance contract money we got. Neither of us is ready for that or losing our jobs."

"Well, where's he going? I want to talk to him," Sandy admitted. She concentrated on Grayson and only half paid attention to Carol's genuine concerns.

"Look," Carol stared at Sandy sternly. "A lot of things have changed and improved in recent years in this country. However, as our work contracts outlined very explicitly, we both agreed to live by some of the old rules 'just in case,' no matter what changes happen. Our company wants no trouble over anything with the officials or the local population. We agreed to live by that."

"You're right. Enough already." Sandy started after Grayson and Carol grabbed her arm. Grayson was far ahead and moving fast.

"Get a grip," Carol said.

Sandy looked at Carol and cocked her head to the side. "A handsome guy—no wedding ring, not too old or young—comes along, and you stop me. Don't be ridiculous. You have been in this heat too long."

"He obviously has other things on his mind. Besides, we're women, and we have to be very careful," Carol reminded Sandy.

"But—" Sandy objected, and Carol interrupted.

"Women here don't have the freedoms we're accustomed to," Carol said sternly. "And especially since we're obligated to follow the old guidelines. Every one of them!"

"How could I forget? Have you forgotten that every male here is married or fresh out of the cradle?" Sandy started to walk and then stopped, looking directly at Carol.

Sandy cocked her head again. "Wait a minute. How would anyone know that guy's not married to one of us?" she asked.

"Here, he could be married to both of us technically. But no public displays of affection are allowed, married or not," Carol stated emphatically.

"Okay, okay. I bet our rescuer has gone to help someone else. Let's shop and at least watch," Sandy said enthusiastically.

Without waiting for an answer, Sandy followed Grayson's path. She stopped momentarily and pretended to look at items along the way. Carol shook her head and huffed but followed Sandy.

"Wait up," Carol yelled. Carol had never seen Sandy move so fast. She caught up to her.

Sandy gave a big smile. "That man is like the Lone Ranger—helping people, then slipping away. My grandpa loves those old reruns," she admitted.

"Looking at an unbuttoned skirt does not exactly qualify him for sainthood. Have you lost your mind?" Carol asked.

Grayson was at a jewelry display but watching the reporters, Drockden and Mark, buying T-shirts. Sandy casually looked at material from a fabric stand while watching Grayson.

"Maybe he has a Tonto friend for you," Sandy said.

"Will you stop it? You sound like a jerk. I'm not interested. I thought you wanted bracelets," Carol replied.

"I do. But I know twenty-four karat when I see it, and this guy's it. I'm not about to miss a great golden opportunity." Sandy grinned.

"Ugh. Seriously? You didn't just say that?" Carol shook her head and laughed.

Drockden and Mark walked down the street on the far end while Grayson discretely followed their every move. Carol and Sandy progressed carefully closer. Drockden and Mark got into their rented car. Then Grayson got in a jeep. Carol spotted a boxing bag in the back seat of the jeep with a drawing of a bull's eye on it.

"What are they doing?" Sandy asked.

"Looks like they're leaving," Carol responded. "Now, let's shop."

"No. We've got to get a taxi," Sandy exclaimed desperately.

"Forget it. We're not following that guy," Carol insisted while Sandy exaggerated a pout. "Look, it's impossible. We've got to be careful, especially being alone."

"We're not alone. We're together," Sandy observed.

"That doesn't count. We're still women in a strict society, with many rules and laws that we agreed to obey, or we wouldn't even be here. We have to be more careful than most! Let's buy some gold," Carol insisted and pulled Sandy toward the merchants.

Carol and Sandy walked to the closest jewelry stand. After considering the choices, Sandy pointed to a bracelet.

"I'd like to buy that one, please," Sandy said.

An Arabic man placed a handful of gold bracelets on a scale. Sandy was confused and looked at the man.

"No. Just that one." Sandy pointed to the piece, but the man did not understand.

Carol shook her head and explained. "They only sell them by weight, not by the piece or design.

"You're kidding. Some of those are majorly ugly." Sandy sighed.

"Hey, at these prices, you take the good with the bad," Carol replied.

Sandy looked at the man and then at the bracelets. She excitedly turned to Carol.

"That's it! The good with the bad. Come on," Sandy said, deciding to not buy gold now. She turned to the man. *"Shukran. Ma Salama."* Thank you and goodbye.

Sandy rushed away, and Carol hurriedly followed. As they quickly passed by the tables, the merchants constantly tried to entice them with their goods to stop.

Carol was frustrated and a bit perplexed. "Where are you going? And what do you mean, 'the good with the bad'?"

"You'll see. Come on; we've got to catch the bus. And a hero," Sandy said as they rushed toward the bus stop.

Chapter Three

CRITICAL COMPROMISE

Carol and Sandy were on a return bus to the compound. Carol looked at Sandy. "I can't believe we left. I thought you wanted to shop."

"Just wait," Sandy said.

From the bus windows, an elaborate complex with luxurious greenery and grass came into view. Three security guards stood sentry at the gate of the entrance station. A vast, beautiful sign sported a gorgeous sunrise and the words: Saudi Sunrise Oil Company's Medical, Rehabilitation, & Financial Compound. Entry by Permit Only. A fence surrounded the entire area.

The bus stopped at the bus stand just outside the gate. Six people exited. All of them retrieved their permits from their purses and wallets. They scanned their passes and quickly entered the compound. A shuttle was waiting inside to take them to their destinations, although most of the bus passengers had parked their private cars in the parking lot inside the gate.

Carol and Sandy got into Sandy's car, not saying much as they traveled. On the way to Sandy's apartment, they drove past the stunning hospital where they worked. The compound was so lush and green, with well-maintained grounds, that it was hard to believe it was still in the desert.

The air conditioning in Sandy's car needed to be serviced, so they had the windows open. To be careful, Carol and Sandy were waiting to talk about important things until they were in Sandy's apartment. They arrived and quickly parked.

For the first time, Sandy beat Carol up the stairs. Carol had never seen Sandy so energetic. Sandy entered her apartment with Carol right behind her. Her home was small but charmingly decorated with trinkets from all of Sandy's travels. Carol sat in a chair as Sandy locked the door.

"Air conditioning and some freedom," Sandy giggled.

"Now that we can talk, tell me what you're thinking," Carol eagerly asked.

Sandy flopped on the couch and unbuttoned her skirt. "Simple—the good with the bad. A long, hot shower and home cooking versus quick showers and packaged food," Sandy said.

"What?" Carol asked, totally confused.

"Years ago, people used to take baked goodies to the military and let GIs shower at their homes. That's not necessary now, but it's worth a shot," Sandy explained and smiled a huge grin.

"We don't even know if he is military," Carol emphatically stated.

Sandy laughed. "Come on. With that haircut, he has to be."

"Well, true. But please, not another idea," Carol groaned.

"Not an idea, a plan. Operation Chocolate Chip Cookie has begun. Our motto: We always get our man. Hopefully, two of them," Sandy declared, giving a salute.

"Give me a break," Carol responded.

Sandy tried to pull Carol up, but she resisted. Sandy kept at it. "Let's get started. I need your help," Sandy pleaded.

"No, this is crazy," Carol scolded. "Let's watch a movie. Aren't you tired from the sweltering heat?"

"I may be tired, but I'm not dead. Now, come on, please," Sandy implored Carol, with her hands folded and giving a pathetic look.

"You're not going to stop, are you?" Carol chuckled.

"No, I'm not," Sandy laughed. "To the kitchen."

Carol gave in and got up. "Just to be clear, I don't want a man," Carol protested vigorously.

"Well, I do, and I need your assistance," Sandy admitted.

They entered the kitchen, and Sandy enthusiastically took dishes from the cabinet. She set them on the counter.

Carol sighed deeply. She was not happy.

"Not all guys are rotten," Sandy declared.

"Wanna bet? You know every long-term boyfriend I've ever had and one fiancé have cheated on me!" Carol replied emphatically.

"That stinks and is terrible. And I'm so sorry you suffered those awful experiences. But you've made some bad choices. It happens. That doesn't mean every guy is bad. There are good ones out there too. Also, there are rotten females. And gold-diggers," Sandy said.

Carol rolled her eyes and sighed again. "You were a cheerleader in high school, weren't you?"

"No, smarty pants. I was a want-to-be like most everybody else," Sandy responded.

"That's the difference. I never ever wanted to be a cheer-leader," Carol replied.

"Way to try to change the subject," Sandy rebuked Carol. "It's not working. Have you ever considered that your dad cheating on your mom has something to do with all this? You said when they split, you hardly ever saw your dad again. And how painful that was. You missed him. It's much easier to constantly try to prove that all guys are bad than to face the fact that your dad was horrible to your mom and you. A complete and utter jerk."

"Well, you're right about that part. I can think of a few more names I'd call him. So, how many psychology rotations did you do?" Carol asked, and they both laughed.

Sandy looked sweetly at Carol. "Well, we both learned in our psych classes that people's reactions to any current situation have way more to do with past experiences than what's actually happening. That's why people respond so differently to the same existing circumstances. So, there are some excellent guys out there. We just have to find them," Sandy said.

Carol smiled at Sandy and affectionately patted her shoulder. "For you, maybe. For me, I'm done. But I'll help keep you out of trouble."

"Well, I want to know why my rescuer was following those guys," Sandy admitted. "It's a mystery and a challenge."

***

Grayson was seated in his parked jeep, pondering and puzzled. He rubbed his face. Then, he took a tiny recorder out of his bag.

"Start of the audio journal on the reporter, Drockden Sorrell. Things are strange. Something is not right..."

Chapter Four

WORTH A TRY

The next day was bright and sunny, as usual. Carol and Sandy left early to embark on the train ride ahead of them to get as close as possible to Eskan Village. The train was preferable to the bus but did not go all the way there.

They loved seeing the sand dunes and the landscape change before their eyes. Today there were many shamals, sandstorms, to watch for miles. They were thankful to not be out in the 115-degree Fahrenheit sweltering heat. However, it was interesting to watch all the panoramic changes redesigning the countryside.

When the train arrived, they took the bus the rest of the way to the transit stand in front of the temporary US Military section at Eskan Village. The total trip took four hours from Riyadh. Some joint Saudi and US Military Training Missions, or USMTMs, were sometimes planned for that area.

"I can't believe you talked me into this trip. It's a long way," Carol complained.

"But it is our best chance of finding out who our rescuer is," Sandy responded.

In the distance, from the window of the parked bus, Sandy saw buff GIs running. She nudged Carol and fanned herself. Carol gave her usual scowl to settle Sandy down.

"I thought we'd never get here," Carol said.

"At least we had air conditioning all the way," Sandy said.

"Well, yes. Or there is no way we would have come," Carol replied.

Two guards watched as Carol and Sandy exited the bus and headed their way. The women walked toward the entrance. Sandy dropped her purse and stopped to get it, holding tightly to the box she carried. Carol waited for Sandy. Then they walked to the guards.

"Hi, Sergeant Brown and Corporal Laurence," Sandy said, reading their name tags while flashing her warm smile.

Both soldiers nodded, and Sergeant Allen Brown gave a slight wave. He appreciated the company.

Sandy continued. "We work for the Oil Company Medical and Rehab Center in Riyadh. We live on the compound, and we're nurses at the hospital."

They showed both guards their compound permits. The guards inspected the permits thoroughly and ran them over a scanner they wore on their belts. Then they scanned both women with wands to check for any metal or weapons.

"It's nice to see Americans out of military uniform. How can we help you ladies?" Sergeant Brown asked as the second guard moved closer.

"We're trying to locate a guy who helped us at the market-place, I mean souk, yesterday in Riyadh," Sandy explained.

Carol finally smiled. "He rescued us, and she made cookies to thank him."

"What's his name or outfit?" Sergeant Brown asked.

Sandy looked at Carol for help. Carol shrugged her shoulders and rubbed her arm.

"Everything happened so fast," Carol said.

"What branch? Army? Marines?" Corporal Craig Laurence asked.

"We don't know," Sandy replied. "But for sure, he has a military haircut, great posture, and is over six feet tall."

Sergeant Brown looked at Sandy and shook his head. "What? That's not much to go on. There are lots of military personnel out here right now," he said.

Carol graphically gestured as she spoke. "We can eliminate ninety percent of them. He's older, forty-ish. Gray on the sides with crow's feet stomping in."

"That's still going to be tough," Sergeant Brown said.

Corporal Laurence leaned in and nodded as he spoke. "Be careful how you phrase that older part. They like being referred to as experienced."

Sandy laughed. "We all get a little sensitive about being long in the tooth. Except her. She doesn't mind being older."

Corporal Laurence scratched his head and raised his eyebrow.

"Not all women are hung up on numbers—age, weight, dress size. She's my hero," Sandy smiled.

Carol shook her head and turned to Sergeant Brown. "Where should we search for this guy? Can we go inside the military area and look for him?"

"Absolutely not at all! No entrance," he said.

At that moment, Colonel Victor Ortega, the Director of Special Ops, drove up in his jeep. He looked inquisitively at the two women. Sergeant Brown walked over to him, saluted, and explained the situation.

Carol started to step off the curb and onto the sand. Corporal Laurence offered his hand as assistance.

"Watch your step, ma'am," Laurence said.

"I'm fine," Carol barked. "I was breathing this heat and walking in this sand while you were still deciding who to take to the prom."

"Carol Renee, shame on you!" Sandy snapped.

Carol took a deep breath and softened her voice. "I'm sorry. I really am. You boys—men and women, I mean—you people do a wonderful job."

"Thank you, ma'am. And don't worry, this heat makes everybody cranky sometimes, ma'am," Laurence said.

Carol grabbed Sandy's arm and whispered. "If this kid calls me 'ma'am' one more time, I'm putting sand fleas down his jockey shorts."

"Be nice," Sandy said. "And behave."

"Sorry. You're right," Carol replied.

The wind blew sand that created a swirl. Everyone always enjoyed seeing the dust devils every time they appeared. Colonel Ortega walked back with Sergeant Brown. The colonel's silver-streaked hair framed his tanned, fifty-year-old face.

"Colonel Ortega, sir," Laurence said, exchanging salutes.

"Good afternoon, ladies," Ortega greeted them. "Sergeant Brown explained your situation. But I see no way of finding the soldier that you're looking for. Even if he is a GI, that is."

Sandy's excitement turned to obvious disappointment. Her shoulders drooped, and her face lost its joy. Carol felt terrible for her and tried to help.

"Please. Can we try? She's not going to let this rest. And I don't want to spend the next month looking for this guy," Carol pleaded.

Ortega looked at Brown. Brown widened his eyes and smiled a mischievous grin.

"What was that description again?" Ortega asked.

"A distinguished, experienced soldier. About six feet tall," Sandy described.

"He isn't a greenhorn," Carol added.

Sandy's enthusiasm returned. "Yeah, he's a little long in the to...torso. A long-waisted gentleman," she said, working to cover her near slip.

"That's not much help," Ortega replied, shaking his head.

"I noticed a heavyweight boxing bag in his jeep," Carol added and gestured the size of the bag with her hands. "And there was a bull's eye painted on it."

Ortega and Brown looked at each other and said, "Grayson!" in unison.

"We've found him. Lt. Colonel Grayson. We'll see that he gets the cookies," Ortega said and reached for the box.

Sandy turned to the side. "Wrong. I mean, we'd like to thank him in person."

"Grayson's not even on the military installation right now," Ortega said.

"Is he back in town?" Sandy asked

Laurence responded. "No. He took a chopper to the Four Seasons Hotel in Riyadh by the private air..." Ortega gave Laurence a dirty look, and he hesitated. "...port."

Colonel Ortega sighed, "Yes, we travel by chopper quite a bit. It is fast, efficient, and timewise most effective. There is a lot of ground to cover. The King Khalid International Airport is about twenty-three miles from Riyadh, but we usually just use the small, private airports. They fit our needs and get us closer to our destinations."

"Well, that certainly makes sense," Sandy said.

Carol took a pad and pen from her purse and handed them to Sandy. She gestured with her hand.

"Write a note. Leave your phone number and the cookies," Carol told Sandy.

Sandy hesitated. She was not sure what to do. Carol motioned again for her to go ahead and write. Trusting Carol, Sandy wrote the note as instructed. She knew they would never have gotten this far without Carol's help.

"Thank you for solving the mystery," Carol said.

"Happy to be of assistance," Ortega replied.

Sandy handed the note and box to Ortega. He smiled and nodded.

"We'll be sure Lt. Colonel Grayson gets the goodies," Ortega said. "That was very thoughtful of you."

"Thanks. And the note too, please," Sandy added.

"Of course," Ortega responded.

They saw a bus coming toward the covered transit shelter area where Sandy and Carol had arrived. Carol grabbed Sandy's arm, very much wanting to depart.

"I guess that's our cue to leave. We have a train to catch. Thank you so much for your help," Carol said.

"Glad we could be of assistance," Colonel Ortega replied.

"Yes. Thank you. And you all get cookies too," Sandy grinned.

Sandy took small packages of cookies from her purse and handed one to each of the three men. Sergeant Brown took his bag with a big smile.

"Thank you," they all responded as Carol and Sandy hurried to the bus.

Brown watched and waved as they left. "Nice meeting you."

Sandy waved as she and Carol rushed to catch the bus. They boarded the vehicle and went straight to the back to sit down. They felt it was more private there.

"I'm happy to be out of the heat," Carol admitted. "And pleased you got your cookies going to your hero."

"Me, too. How did you know that was a boxing bag?" Sandy asked. "I thought it was his dirty laundry."

"Easy. My brother was the golden-gloves champ in college. I'm glad you found out who your rescuer is," Carol replied.

"That was a great idea to leave the cookies, so we don't have to carry them to the hotel," Sandy said.

"We left the cookies so we wouldn't have to go to the hotel," Carol responded adamantly.

"Oh, come on. Of course, we're going to the hotel. Don't be such a stick-in-the-sand," Sandy said with a huge grin.

Carol gave her stern look. "You've got to be kidding," Carol snarled.

Sandy pushed Carol's shoulder with her hand. "We can nap on the train on the way. It'll be fun and an adventure," she smiled.

***

Colonel Ortega was gone. Sergeant Brown ate one of his cookies.

"This is good," Brown said.

"Yeah, they are. Mine are long gone," Laurence replied.

Brown handed his baggie with the last cookie to Corporal Laurence.

"Here, put this with all those caramel popcorn balls you eat from the mess tent. It's way better," Brown said.

Laurence frowned. "Hey, those popcorn balls are my favorite. I hope the hotel keeps 'em comin.'" Then he took the cookie out of the package. "What's 'long in the tooth' mean?" he asked.

Brown laughed and responded. "You know, like elephants, bobcats, whatever grow longer teeth the older they get."

Laurence jokingly looked at Brown's teeth. "Would you like to borrow my file, sir?"

Brown smiled. "Experience, savvy, charm. There are many benefits of age."

"Rank?" Laurence asked.

"Yeah. Absolutely," Brown replied with a grin.

Chapter Five

WHAT GIVES?

Sandy and Carol arrived at the Four Seasons Hotel. It was mammoth and gorgeous with quite a unique, modern design. Everything was exquisite. Sandy thought of all the luxury they were experiencing and how incredible this building was. Carol thought of all the poor people whose lives could be helped if these riches were put to better use. Sandy almost tripped but caught herself. Carol fought back a chuckle and coughed to cover it up. Sandy pushed the revolving door as she and Carol entered the lobby.

The interior of the lobby was as lavish as the exterior. There were three enormous chandeliers with a huge fountain in the center. Gilded mirrors lined the walls, and plush, red velvet furniture surrounded the grand piano.

"This must be what Paradise looks like," Sandy observed.

"Actually, I'm hoping for better," Carol admitted and laughed.

People milled and mingled. All of them were smiling as if they did not have a care in the world. Sandy broke the surreal feeling.

"I wish we could wear something else. I feel like a mummy in these long dresses," Sandy complained.

"I don't want to hear it. We're wasting our time off with this nonsensical chase," Carol said sternly.

Sandy grimaced. "Sshhh. We're just here for dinner. Anyway, many of the reporters are probably here, too. Or at the Al Faisaliah Hotel. I want to find out as much as we can."

"Brilliant deduction, since most of the reporters usually frequent here, trying to catch celebrities," Carol said.

"Get happy," Sandy replied. "You always tell me that happiness is a choice. So, choose it." Sandy gasped. "Ahhh. Is that Grayson over there reading the newspaper?"

"Get real. You'd think he was Elvis or something. Cut it out already," Carol said in frustration.

"He's better than Elvis. He's alive," Sandy replied and excitedly walked toward Grayson.

Carol followed. "Remember, no touching!" she warned.

Sandy hurried. "Well, hello there. Have you seen any unbuttoned skirts lately? I mean, well, I just..." Sandy stuttered and panicked.

Carol came to the rescue. "Wanted to thank you again for coming to our aid yesterday."

Sandy breathed a sigh of relief. She searched for words but was too enamored with Grayson's good looks and had trouble thinking of anything to say. Grayson listened.

Finally, Sandy said, "Yes, thank you."

"You're welcome, but it was nothing."

"'It' saved us," Sandy said, and her beautiful smile gleamed.

Mark and Drockden exited the hotel restaurant and entered the lobby. Grayson intently watched as they walked toward the door. Very unexpectedly, Grayson stood.

"Nice to see you again, ladies. Stay safe," Grayson said as he walked away and went to the corner of the lobby.

Mark and Drockden stopped in the gift shop and perused the T-shirts. Trying not to be noticed, Grayson discreetly picked up a brochure.

"Again, he's interested in those two guys instead of me," Sandy said in frustration.

"Maybe he's gay," Carol suggested.

"No way," Sandy responded.

"You're right. Something's up," Carol conceded.

Subtly, Sandy watched Grayson. "I think he's taking pictures of those guys."

Carol turned slowly to see. Grayson had a small camera aimed at Drockden and Mark behind his brochure.

"You're right. Maybe they're spies or something," Carol said.

"Maybe. But one thing's certain, those guys are the quickest route to Grayson," Sandy said, heading toward the gift shop.

"Oh, no," Carol responded.

Sandy walked directly to Mark and Drockden in the gift shop.

"Excuse me. Have you ever tried the food in there?" Sandy asked and pointed to the restaurant.

Mark smiled and returned the charm. "Yes, repeatedly. Not that it's great, but it's close."

Carol joined them. She looked around, trying to be nonchalant.

"What's the best dish on the menu?" Sandy asked.

"Oh, that stuff we had the other day. What's it called?" Drockden asked.

"I couldn't pronounce it even if I could remember. But we have some time; we'll show you," Mark responded.

"Great," Sandy said enthusiastically.

"Our pleasure," Mark replied. "By the way, I'm Mark and this is Drockden. And you are?" Mark put his hand out toward Sandy.

"Oh, I'm Sandy, and this is Carol." Sandy motioned to Carol.

Grayson watched in shock. He was having trouble believing what just transpired but kept watching, as hidden as possible. Mark paid for his T-shirt.

"So why are you guys here? With that hair, you can't be military," Sandy said, and Carol winced.

"We're reporters, here to cover the upcoming wedding of the Saudi Prince," Mark said.

"And all the celebrities and big wigs attending the celebration," Drockden added.

"To get good scoops, you must be ahead of the action. So, we're here waiting for something to happen," Mark explained.

"So, what celebrities are coming?" Sandy asked.

"Who knows? It's all top secret," Drockden responded.

"Like the number of US troops visiting in the country. It's impossible to find out how many are here," Mark said. "Some have come from Bahrain, some for Qatar, and some from the United Arab Emirates, that I know of. All for the wedding festivities. I think they're here because there is major chatter going around that something bad is going to happen. It seems like they are preparing to help out to keep everything and everyone safe. The US is good at intel and clandestine stuff."

Drockden laughed. "Mark tried counting the number of soldiers, but that was futile. They keep things very low-key and guarded. Have you seen the Royal Saudi Air Force? They are majorly imposing! Last I heard, they are the third-largest fleet in the world. If it hasn't changed, the US is number one and Japan number two."

"We have seen the Royal Saudi Air Force. And you are right; they are very impressive. Unbelievably so," Carol agreed.

Mark took his bag from the clerk, and the four walked toward the restaurant. Meanwhile, Grayson had repositioned himself to be more concealed and watched every move.

"So, the celebrity watch continues," Mark said.

"Getting scoops sounds exciting," Sandy replied.

"Everybody thinks so. But waiting around is boring. And we spend lots of time waiting," Drockden admitted.

Mark held up his T-shirt bag and pointed. "Now I'm collecting T-shirts. Sad, eh?" he said and pointed to Drockden. "And he's started selling TV satellite dishes."

Sandy stopped walking. "If you're looking for something to do, how about golf?"

"I love golf," Mark said. "I used to think this place was just one big sand trap, but this country has taken off with golf courses. From what I read, they have some made with grass and some made with sand."

"We work for the Oil Company Medical and Rehab Center in Riyadh. We live on the compound, and we're nurses at the hospital. There's a golf course on the compound for the expats—or expatriates, working here from other countries. It's beautiful. You'll see," Sandy explained.

"We'd love to. That would be great," Mark responded, sounding excited.

"Decades ago, when the Americans first helped the Saudis get their oil company started here, they built a golf course in Dhahran," Sandy said. "But now the Saudis build lots of courses. Great ones, too."

"I learned about some of those golf courses in my research," Mark admitted. "The last I heard, Jack Nicklaus, one of the greatest golf champions and course designers in the world, is creating one enormous course here. Somewhere. How long were the Americans here under contract?"

"Oh, for many years. I think, like ninety-nine or something. A long time. The Americans and the Saudi Arabians worked well together. Come by tomorrow, and you'll see a great golf course in person," Sandy declared.

"This I've got to see," Mark responded.

"We'll leave civilian guest passes at the main gate for you. Then an escort will bring you to my apartment," Sandy said.

Drockden extended his arm to Sandy in a gentlemanly fashion to enter the restaurant. Carol stopped Sandy from taking his arm. "No touching, remember?" Carol said sternly.

"Oh, thanks. She keeps me straight," Sandy admitted, as she lowered her arm.

"I forgot too." Drockden confessed, as they entered the restaurant single file. Grayson, still hidden, was shocked as he watched.

***

The following day, Sandy was in her apartment, and there was a knock at the door. She was slightly panicked. Sandy forced herself to open the door, and Carol entered carrying a grocery bag.

"Boy, am I glad it's you. I need to get a peephole put in the front door. I was afraid Mark and Drockden beat you here," Sandy said.

"I've been telling you for months to get a peephole. You can't be too careful nowadays. I picked up the sodas you wanted," Carol said. "And they're cold."

"Thank you. That's a big help. I straightened the apartment. They'll be here any minute. I still say we should have had them come to your place. It's so much nicer," Sandy admitted.

"No. This is your show, dearie," Carol smiled.

The phone rang. As Sandy raced to the phone, Carol put the bag in the kitchen on the table.

"They better not cancel," Sandy said as she picked up the receiver.

"Hello. Oh, hello."

Carol walked into the living room. Sandy turned the mouthpiece of the receiver up and pointed to it.

"It's Grayson," she whispered.

Sandy nervously fanned herself, and Carol quietly laughed.,

"You're welcome," Sandy said, and Carol gestured two thumbs- up.

"I'm glad you like the cookies. Listen, you have an open invitation to use my shower any time," Sandy told Grayson. Carol's mouth dropped, and then Sandy's mouth dropped. She put her hand to her open mouth.

"No, we don't really know those guys, but they're coming to play golf. Do you know them?" she asked.

There was a knock at the door. Sandy's and Carol's eyes both widened.

"I'll get it," Carol whispered and motioned with her hand.

Carol opened the door. It was Mark and Drockden, accompanied by one of the compound escorts.

The escort was in full uniform, and he was clutching a clipboard. "I'm looking for Carol Page and Sandra Morrison. You have to sign for your two civilian guests."

"I'm Carol Page." She took the pen to sign, and Sandy joined them. There were photographs of Mark and Drockden at the top of the sheet.

"Somebody, one of you, must accompany both men at all times," the escort instructed. "And your guests must be off the compound no later than seven p.m. tonight. Check and initial the boxes indicating you understand the rules that are listed. Then sign on the line at the bottom."

"We understand," Carol said.

Both girls did as instructed, and the escort immediately left.

"Come in." Sandy motioned Mark and Drockden inside, and they entered.

"They are super picky," Mark said. "We filled out some paperwork with our international credentials, so it won't be so hard to get in here next time—at least, I hope it won't be. This complex is much nicer than I expected."

"We're glad you made it," Sandy said.

"Hey, how can you be wearing shorts?" Drockden asked Sandy. "Isn't that taboo?"

"It is. Absolutely," Sandy replied. "We can only wear them on the compound. And not close to any compound boundaries where we could be seen from the outside. To be safe, we just wear them at home. We'd get fired in a heartbeat if we were ever seen wearing them."

Carol raised her eyebrow. "That is, if we lived that long. We'd likely get stoned to death, like in Biblical times."

***

Grayson was at his temporary office desk and on the telephone. The room was sparsely furnished and had only maps on the walls.

"I need you to do a background check for me on two American females," Grayson said and looked at his notes on the desk. "Yes. Immediately," he responded.

Chapter Six

PROGRESS VERSUS PROBLEMS

At Sandy's apartment, Mark and Drockden were seated on the couch. Sandy and Carol were in the chairs facing the sofa. They had sodas in a bottle and a friendly chat.

Sandy smiled. "We can do things on the compound that we can't do anywhere else, like wear shorts and keep our heads and hair uncovered."

"Can you believe that?" Carol said, with outrage in her voice. "When I first came here, women were not even allowed to drive at all. I think they lifted that ban in 2018 or so, which is good. Some progress. Or maybe it was 2017. I'm not sure. Although, we could always drive just on the compound. But we still only drive on the compound to be safe because our company is ridiculously cautious to avoid getting into any trouble."

Sandy gave Carol a dirty look. "Our company is extremely cautious. Laws that change can be changed back quickly. Also, even though a law has changed, sometimes the population does not agree with it. So, we do everything on the conservative side. The company wants no trouble whatsoever with the law or the citizenry."

"I read about the driving part in my research," Mark said. "Did you know that even though there are incredible trains and buses here, ninety-five percent of the population still drive their own cars?"

"We usually take the bus because it's cheaper than the train, and that gives us more travel money to visit other countries," Sandy said. "But both systems are impressive. And there are taxis and Uber, and now even women Uber drivers."

Mark looked shocked. "Wow. That I didn't know. However, I found it interesting that non-Muslims cannot access the train station in Mecca. They are not allowed. But I was surprised at some of the restrictions."

"Me, too," Sandy admitted. "I had to get used to a couple of things. Absolutely no alcohol allowed and no cussing."

"I know, no drugs or pornography either," Drockden added as he settled back in his seat. "But those are good things."

"Those are easy. I didn't do them back home," Sandy said.

Mark laughed. "But the no alcohol and no cussing were a challenge, eh?"

Sandy smiled, and Carol came to her rescue again, as she often did.

"What surprised me the most when I first got here was when I saw pictures cut out of news magazines because they showed female shoulders uncovered. What in the world is sexy about shoulders?" Carol asked.

"Not exactly my idea of porn, for sure," Mark replied. "But they've lifted lots of restrictions and made huge changes in the last decade. In 2013, women were finally allowed to ride bicycles. But the Crown Prince Mohammed bin Salman Al Saud, or 'MBS' as he's called, has done some great stuff since he's been in charge. So far, I like this guy. In 2017, the first woman was chosen to chair the Saudi Arabian stock exchange. Now, women can even join the military, and, like you said, Sandy, women can be Uber drivers. And in 2019, they banned marriage if you're under 18 for both genders."

"That would be a great law for every country," Carol said. "Teenagers don't necessarily make the right decisions. And even if parents have to sign for the marriage, not everybody has good parents. In general, minors cannot sign contracts, but they let them marry. That never made sense to me."

"With the high divorce rate, it looks like many people make bad decisions. Young and old," Sandy laughed, and everyone else joined, too.

"But you're right. That would be a good law in many places," Drockden added. "Saudi Arabia even has a Committee for the Propagation of Virtue and the Prevention of Vice. That would be good to have in other countries, too."

"Wow," Sandy said. "Not many places promote virtue nowadays. That's interesting. But it can also be extreme."

"I hope MBS ends up being as good as one of my favorites, King Abdullah II of Jordan," Mark said. "He never seemed to want power, only to do the right things for his country and his people. And right things in general. He is a real hero and a genuinely good man. You can't say that about many people nowadays. We need more like him in positions of power.

"MBS is quite the innovator." Mark paused a moment, then continued enthusiastically, "Oh, and I remembered that as of 2021, women are now allowed to live alone in Saudi Arabia. They have made some big strides. But the coolest thing is the mirrored glass city MBS has planned, ' The Line,' being built in Neom. It will be taller than the Empire State Building, something like thirteen square miles, and home to well over a million people. No cars, no emissions, and 95-100 percent renewables. And also, I'm dying to see how the LIV Golf Tour he started turns out. I thought the LIV was like live, but it's the Roman Numeral for fifty-four. So, there will be fifty-four golf holes somehow, I think. It's just incredible what he's doing! But only time will let us know if he is as good as he comes across with all the changes and innovations. We'll see. With time, people have a way of showing who they really are, even when they don't want to."

Carol nodded her head. "That is so true. But they have improved many things. It is way better than when I first came, eleven years ago. But what I don't get is when I go to Europe or back to the States, I can't believe how much worse things are. Especially for women. Way more skin is shown everywhere. And they use sex and bodies to sell everything!"

"Well, that's because it works," Mark replied, shrugging his shoulders.

"But it gets worse every year," Carol said adamantly. "Women may be oppressed here, but from what I see, in other countries, they're exploited—"

Sandy cut her off. Sandy shook her head and waved her hands dismissively.

"Enough already. We're not here to solve social injustice! Or anything. We're supposed to be playing golf. Are you ready?" Sandy asked.

"Yes, I want to play some golf," Mark replied. "That's something super to write home about."

"I'll change, and we're on our way. We'll catch a bus, which is easier than driving the car anyway. Plus, the air conditioning is great," Sandy responded and hurried to the bedroom.

Carol picked up a camera from the table and asked, "Pictures after golf?"

***

The sun shone brightly, and the golf course was surprisingly beautiful. The grass was very lush, and palm trees were plentiful. There were nicely carved wooden signs that said 18th Green. They had truly enjoyed playing the eighteen holes together, even though it was extremely hot. Mark, Sandy, and Drockden posed by one of the signs. Carol aimed the camera to take a picture.

"Great round of golf, guys. Now smile," Carol said.

They all smiled and posed. Carol snapped several shots.

"This is incredible. It's hard to believe this is Saudi Arabia," Drockden said.

"Are you sure you got the pictures with the palm trees?" Mark asked.

"I got it. I got several. Did you know yummy dates come from palm trees and are extremely healthy?" Carol asked.

"I didn't know that," Mark replied.

Carol smiled and pointed left. "Now you guys walk that way, and I'll get a distance shot."

Sandy walked backward and tripped over her foot. Mark caught her and helped her stand, then quickly let go.

"Oh, thanks," Sandy said, slightly embarrassed.

"Sure," Mark responded. Sandy beamed, noticing how cute Mark was in the sunlight.

"You said there's a restaurant here for an early dinner?" Drockden asked.

"Yes," Sandy replied.

"Great, our treat," Drockden said.

Carol signaled with her arm. "Well, let's hurry. I'm melting in this heat."

"We'll be back in air conditioning soon. Some of the poor soldiers never get a break from the temperature," Sandy replied.

"Last picture," Carol said and motioned them back.

Carol walked in one direction. Sandy, Mark, and Drockden walked in the other direction and posed.

"Wave," Carol instructed. She snapped the picture, and Mark kept waving.

***

Drockden held the restaurant door open and indicated for Sandy, Carol, and Mark to enter. The group enthusiastically went into the air-conditioned compound restaurant closest to the golf course and anticipated a great meal. Mark gestured to the waiter. The waiter walked over and led them to a table. They all sat down but Sandy.

"Hey, guys. I'll be back," Sandy said and headed to the ladies' room.

***

Grayson entered a building marked Temporary US Military Section, Eskan Village. It was near Riyadh, where the Saudis and the US sometimes planned joint training missions. The US Military Training Missions, or USMTM, were intricately designed and helped both nations and, in reality, the world.

Grayson walked down the hall to the last door; the nameplate beside the door read: Sergeant James Richards, Communication Specialist. Grayson entered, closing the door behind him. Satellite dishes and parts lay strewn across the various tables around the room. James, sitting among the clutter, took off his headphones when he saw Grayson. Behind James, large radio equipment was connected and set up.

"Were you able to get locals to buy the satellite dishes from Drockden for you?" Grayson asked.

"Yes, sir. No one suspected a thing. The dishes were so cheap that this guy was practically giving them away. I bought four," James replied and gestured to the equipment on the tables.

"What'd you find?" Grayson asked.

"Four perfectly normal satellite dishes."

"What?" Grayson responded in complete surprise.

"That's it," James reported. "I disconnected every circuit board, completely dismantled every inch, and found nothing abnormal."

"Well, something's not right," Grayson said with significant disappointment. "Guess it's just not the satellite dishes. Thanks."

"Sure. Anytime," James replied.

"Still keep this just between us," Grayson requested.

"Definitely. Well, you, me, and Betsy." James pointed to the radio behind him, and Grayson smiled.

"Well, you and Betsy keep an ear out. You're the only ones I trust. Strange things are happening, and we've got to figure this out as soon as possible," Grayson said and headed toward the door.

"You got it, sir," James replied.

***

The restaurant bustled with people from all walks of life. Carol, Mark, and Drockden were seated and studying their menus.

Carol paused. "Most Muslims are reasonable people. But there's a small percentage of extremists who promote violence."

"I know that. But you can find some of those in almost every group," Mark replied.

The waiter returned, and Mark explained they were not yet ready to order. "We need some more time, please," Mark said. The waiter smiled, nodded, and walked toward the kitchen.

"Maybe the extremists feel that what's important is the next life, and whatever must be endured here doesn't matter," Drockden suggested.

"Doesn't matter?" Carol objected. "Tell that to the fatherless children and mothers who have buried sons. This life does matter. You're infuriating!"

"And you're irritating," Drockden responded.

Sandy returned and smacked Carol's shoulder. "Have you lost your minds? You can't discuss this here; you'll get us all deported."

Mark rose and pulled out Sandy's chair. She smiled and sat down.

"Let's order and discuss something safe," Sandy said. "Sports. That's safe. Who are the basketball and football heroes nowadays? I'm clueless."

"If you're talking real heroes, Enes Kanter Freedom gets my vote," Mark nodded emphatically.

***

There was an airfield in the distance. A helicopter took off smoothly but then swayed violently and lost control. The pilot fought to regain stability. The swaying started again. They almost crashed but finally managed to land safely. The crew exited the chopper, shaken to the core.

"Whew!" the pilot sighed. "That'll make you kiss the ground."

***

Sandy and Carol looked very tired as they dragged themselves into Sandy's apartment. It had been a long, hot day. It was late, and they had just gotten away from Mark and Drockden. The guys barely made their deadline of being off the compound by seven.

"I didn't think we'd ever get rid of them," Carol said and closed the door.

Sandy looked at Carol. "So, why is it that Grayson doesn't need an escort to come here?"

"At his military rank, he's good to go all over this compound and even drive his vehicle anywhere here," Carol said. "Oh, and he has no time restrictions. I'm sure he has a much higher clearance than any of the escorts or guards. The main gate keeps rigorous electronic records. And think about it; it's way wiser to let him on the compound than you or me."

They both laughed. "Well, good point," Sandy said. "But Grayson's on his way, and I don't have time to shower. I'm all hot and sweaty. Real attractive, eh?"

"What was it you said to me? Think of the poor GIs. They're hot and sweaty all the time."

Sandy threw a small couch pillow at Carol, and she caught it.

"I bet Grayson smells so bad that he won't even notice your stench," Carol said.

"Aww, Thanks. Then as soon as he's showered, I'm doomed," Sandy sighed.

"Just spray some perfume," Carol suggested.

"Lysol's more like it," Sandy replied.

"I've got to hand it to you. With all the attention Mark gave you, I figured Grayson was history," Carol observed.

"Mark's cute, but—"

There was a knock at the door. Sandy panicked.

"Oh no. You've got to keep Grayson busy. I'll hurry," Sandy said.

Carol nodded and chuckled. Sandy ran out of the room, and then Carol opened the door.

"Hi, Lt. Colonel Grayson. Come in," Carol said, motioning him inside.

Grayson entered carrying a duffle bag and looked very dashing in his dress uniform. "Thank you. I appreciate this," he said.

"Please, sit down," Carol motioned. Grayson sat in a chair, and Carol sat on the couch.

Sandy called from the bedroom, "I'll be right there."

"We just got in," Carol said.

"So, how was the golf?" Grayson asked.

"Hot. But I guess you already knew that," she chuckled.

"Yes. There's lots of hot around here," he replied.

"It's got to be hard for soldiers to live as you guys do."

"Part of the job. It can be hard but not nearly as tough as life sometimes gets," Grayson said.

"Wow. That's deep. I'd—"

Sandy made an entrance wearing a flowing, knee-length dress.

Using his good manners and innate charm, Grayson stood.

"I'm so glad you could come," Sandy said, smiling. "You look very nice all decked out in your uniform."

"Well, thank you. I just came from a high-level meeting. You look very nice yourself," Grayson said, returning the compliment.

***

Mark was in his hotel room, adding to his T-shirt collection hanging on the rods of the closed curtain. He placed the hanger of the latest purchase with the rest. Drockden was irritated.

"So, what do you think?" Mark asked.

"That you're annoying," Drockden responded.

"Everything and everybody annoy you. Nothing new there. Well, I think both girls are cute," Mark admitted.

"It figures. I'm going to bed," Drockden said.

"Already, again?" Mark asked.

***

Sandy and Carol were seated on the couch. Grayson looked distinguished sitting in the chair.

"Would you like some lemon cake with ice cream? It's delicious," Sandy said.

"Ice cream sounds good," Grayson replied.

"I'll get it," Carol volunteered. She stood and walked toward the kitchen. She hoped to give Sandy and Grayson some time alone.

"Thanks," Sandy said to Carol and turned toward Grayson. "So, what's your first name? What do your friends call you?"

"Grayson, ma'am. I just go by Grayson."

Sandy was extremely nervous and started to fidget. She twiddled the hem of her dress around her fingers.

"So, you spent the afternoon with Hillsborough and Sorrell?" Grayson asked.

Sandy let go of the hem. "Is that Mark and Drockden?" She questioned.

"Yes. Sorry," Grayson smiled.

"Yeah, we did. We went out to eat after golfing too. And we were at the restaurant forever, it seemed," Sandy admitted.

"I'd like to see this golf course you're talking about." Grayson leaned forward and put his hands on his knees.

"Well, not tomorrow. I unexpectedly have to work a double shift. A friend got sick. And a lot of people are on vacation."

"That time of the year, huh?" Grayson said.

"We get lots of vacation time," Sandy admitted. "They make us get away by leaving the country, so we'll stay with the job and not quit. Rest and recovery, you know."

"It's important. So, why are you here?" Grayson asked.

"The pay's great and tax-free. You can't beat that. I'm still paying off my college loans and can do it a lot faster by being here. Plus, now, I've learned I like world travel."

Sandy flared her dress across the couch. "It took me six years to get through college. And it looked like it would be at least another ten to pay off the loans until I decided to work here."

"You should have considered the military. There are great educational benefits," Grayson said.

Carol entered carrying a tray and served the ice cream.

"Here we go. Even sprinkles, if you want," Carol said.

"Thank you," Grayson replied, taking the bowl of ice cream but no sprinkles.

"Now Carol stays for a completely different reason. She subtly promotes the idea of women's rights. I just hope she doesn't get hung or something," Sandy confided.

"Very funny. I'll get sodas," Carol said as she returned to the kitchen.

"I embarrassed her. But she cares. I admire her for it. There aren't many like that nowadays," Sandy said.

"Sure there are. Lots of them on the dunes at the other side of the airstrip," Grayson said.

Sandy did not know how to respond and remained quiet. Carol returned, and the conversation continued, lasting for an hour. There were empty dishes on the coffee table. Sandy and Carol were still on the couch, and Grayson was in the chair holding his glass.

Sandy sighed. "We get our work schedule tomorrow. Then we'll know when we can take you golfing."

"Okay. Sounds good," Grayson replied.

"So, how is it that you know Mark and Drockden?" Sandy asked.

"I don't. Does that offer of a long, hot shower still stand? I haven't had one of those since I got here." Grayson finished his soda.

"Of course," Sandy responded.

Grayson stood and started to pick up his dish.

"Just leave it. We'll get the dishes," Sandy insisted. "But thank you."

"Well, thank you for everything," he said. Grayson's satchel clanked as he picked it up. "I won't be too long. I have a night maneuver to watch."

Grayson discretely measured his steps as he walked to the bathroom. Sandy watched Grayson walk. The bathroom door closed.

"Looks like you asked the wrong question," Carol said.

"I guess so. What should we do?"

"We? I think you should stop playing games and tell him we saw him following the reporters." Carol put both hands out and up. "Come on now."

"If I say that, Grayson will know we were following him."

"Well, we were."

"I don't want him to know," Sandy pleaded.

"Just make it like we wanted to thank him. Not that you're after his bod," Carol chuckled.

"Shhh! He might hear you," Sandy whispered.

Carol and Sandy started laughing and could not stop. They tried to keep quiet so Grayson wouldn't hear. Carol gestured for Sandy to quieten. Sandy covered her face with a pillow, but they both kept laughing. Tears of laughter streamed down their cheeks. Finally, Carol took deep breaths with a huge smile and motioned for Sandy to do the same. At last, they composed themselves.

Carol became serious. "Grayson made a statement earlier about life that makes me wonder what he's been through."

***

The shower was running in Sandy's bathroom. Grayson was still fully dressed. He quietly stood on the toilet, removed the bathroom vent grate, and carefully took a small, round device from his bag. Using a corded wire, he slowly and quietly pushed a microphone down the duct toward the living room. Grayson retrieved two more microphones. He slowly pushed one toward the dining room and then placed the other one immediately inside the bathroom vent.

Chapter Seven

CHARMING DECEPTION

With perfect posture, Colonel Victor Ortega entered one of the many aircraft hangars. He walked up to the plane closest to the soldier. Staff Sergeant Tony Arseneault greeted Colonel Ortega and saluted. The colonel returned the salute.

"So, what seems to be the problem here?" Ortega asked.

Arseneault affectionately patted his plane. "Sir, she can't take off. Her props aren't right. She can taxi, but she can't fly."

One of the other soldiers, Lance Corporal Logan Carson, got on the platform with a long vacuum hose. He looked at Arseneault.

"What's wrong?" Ortega asked.

"There's sand in there, sir," Arseneault replied and turned to Carson. "Hey, Carson. Wait."

"Our aircraft have faced problems with wind sand for years," Ortega explained.

"Sir," Arseneault said respectfully. "Look at this." Arseneault got on the platform, reached into the turbine housing, and pulled out multiple hands full of sand.

Ortega pensively placed his fist under his chin and stared. "This is more than wind sand."

***

Nurse Callie Adams was writing at the nurses' station desk. Sandy dragged herself over and sat in the chair beside her.

"You look beat," Adams said.

"I am. I hope I can make it till the end of the shift," Sandy confessed.

"Just two more hours. Then you can come back tomorrow and do it again. Double shifts stink," Adams smiled.

"Don't remind me. The desert isn't going to kill us; the nursing coordinator is," Sandy declared.

Sandy put her elbow on the counter and supported her head with her hand. She fought falling asleep right there.

"They promise this double-duty won't last long. Administration is supposed to bring in some new nurses," Adams responded.

"Oh, good, this is worse than the military. At least they get great benefits," Sandy said as her eyes closed.

"Yeah, and tents and twenty-mile hikes in hundred-plus degree heat. Also, only a fraction of our pay," Adams reminded Sandy.

"Great point," Sandy replied.

Carol walked up and gave a huge grin. "Request completed as planned," she said.

Sandy immediately perked up, and her eyes widened with excitement. She grabbed Carol by the elbow and pulled her away from the nurses' station.

"What happened? Give me details," Sandy said enthusiastically.

"When Grayson called about golfing, I told him we'd get pictures of him as we did for Mark and Drockden," Carol explained.

"Then what?" Sandy asked.

"A thousand questions. Were the pictures printed? Where were they taken? Any close shots?" Carol said.

"I knew it!" Sandy exclaimed.

Two nurses walked by Sandy and Carol. They moved farther down the hall for privacy.

"This confirms he's after those guys. You should have told him about the photos last night," Carol firmly stated to Sandy, pointing her finger.

"You saw how he reacted when I asked how he knew Mark and Drockden. I didn't dare bring them up again," Sandy admitted.

"Yeah, true. Well, Grayson offered to pick up the camera. He said he could get the pictures developed in a higher quality for free," Carol said, nodding her head and smiling.

***

The hotel was even more magnificent at night with all the spectacular lights and water fountains. The night before, there was no moonlight and it was very dark at the perimeter. Grayson had stayed for hours with great cover, trying to follow Drockden. He discretely hid behind trees and barriers and mounds of sand.

However, today it was much earlier and not yet dark, so Grayson sat in the parked car even farther away and observed the hotel's entrance. He was in camouflage gear and a cap. There were surveillance goggles on the seat next to him. Grayson waited, knowing it was a long shot that Drockden would appear at this time of day. He scrutinized the area intently. Finally, Drockden arrived at the hotel in a taxi and entered.

Grayson checked the time, staying as long as he possibly could. Drockden never exited the hotel. His watch alarmed, and Grayson had to leave.

***

Carol and Sandy were walking down the hall to Sandy's apartment.

"I don't know why I had to come; Grayson picking up the camera gives you a perfect chance to be alone," Carol said.

"But he makes me so nervous. I know I'll do something stupid," Sandy said and shook both hands frantically.

"And you want me here to watch it," Carol chuckled.

"No, I want you here to fix it. Who knows how long I have?" Sandy said.

"All right, I'm here. Relax; you have lots of extra time since our meeting was so short. We're way early," Carol replied.

"Pam agreed to work the double for me tomorrow. It'll only cost me my television for a month," Sandy said sadly, and Carol looked surprised. "But Grayson's worth it," Sandy grinned.

Sandy and Carol immediately entered the apartment.

Carol laughed. "We need to talk about the obsessive side of your personality."

"So, how many psychology rotations did you do?" Sandy asked jokingly.

A noise came from the kitchen. Sandy looked at Carol, and both hurried to the kitchen doorway.

Grayson was working with fingerprinting equipment. Sandy was excited to see Grayson, but Carol was shocked.

"Hope you don't mind; the door was unlocked, so I let myself in," Grayson said.

"Any time. Excuse the mess. I didn't get to the dishes. Let's go to the living room," Sandy replied.

Carol watched in astonishment as they passed by her. "'Excuse the mess?' Half of it's his!" Carol said emphatically.

"Carol, ssshhh," Sandy responded.

"Listen, you son-of-a-biscuit-maker; I want to know exactly what this is about. Just who do you think you are breaking into Sandy's home?" Carol angrily stated and went toward the telephone.

"Let me try to explain," Grayson said.

"You'd better do more than try. I can't stand cat-and-mouse games. What Sandy's been doing is childish and annoying, but this is criminal!" Carol declared.

"Please, ladies, let's sit down and talk this out," Grayson said calmly, motioning to the living room seats.

"Ugh, okay," Carol replied.

Carol sat in a chair and folded her arms in a defensive position. Grayson and Sandy sat on the couch.

"I just got here early and thought I'd surprise you ladies with my special treat," Grayson said.

Carol raised her arms in the air. "What's that? Bull a la mode? I know fingerprinting equipment when I see it. We want the truth. Now!" Carol demanded through gritted teeth.

"This has nothing to do with you. I promise," Grayson said ardently.

Carol repeatedly gestured to Sandy and herself. "It does now. Breaking and entering puts us right in the middle," Carol replied.

"There are things I can't say. National Security's at risk," Grayson said.

Carol looked Grayson straight in the eye. "I would say, what nation? But I had you checked out with a friend from the Pentagon. So, I believe you, but I will still call the Compound Police if you—"

Grayson's eyebrows raised, and he partially stood. His frustration was evident, but he forced himself to sit back down again.

"The Pentagon?" Grayson asked. "But this is dangerous. I don't want to get you involved. Or anyone, for that matter. I have no idea how bad this is."

"We'll take our chances," Carol said emphatically. "We saw you following Mark and Drockden. And your camera. That's when Sandy decided to take pictures of them when we were golfing. To help you."

"So, you've been doing some spying of your own," Grayson replied.

"Well, yes, but we don't know why," Carol admitted. "Look, after living abroad, we love America and freedom a whole lot more than most. Many people back home take our liberties for granted. If there's a way we can help, we want to."

Carol stood up. She got earnest. "But I'll tell you what we won't do. We won't just forget about this." Carol glared at Grayson. "We want the truth. We'll trade the pictures in that camera and a breaking and entering charge for the facts."

"I don't have much choice now, do I?" Grayson admitted.

"No. But you can trust us, both of us," Carol said and sat back down in the chair.

"I know that. I had both of you checked out, too," Grayson said with a grin.

"Investigated by the military? Ah," Sandy added. She put her hands on her forehead and leaned back against the couch.

"Don't change the subject. Why are you after Mark and Drockden?" Carol forcefully asked.

"I'm not after Mark, just Drockden," Grayson declared.

"Why?" Carol probed.

"Picture this. Twenty years ago, the Marines were scanning a building. I saw a booby trap wire, a tripwire, coming from the floor just as young Drockden's foot was about to snag it. 'Watch out, Drockden!' I called. Then I shoved him backward, knocking him to the floor. The Sergeant ordered everybody out and the bomb squad in. The squad brought out the bomb, and we watched as they detonated it. There was a huge explosion. Drockden looked at me, his eyes filled with tears. We shook hands and then hugged." Grayson's eyes teared up.

"So, you saved Drockden's life?" Carol asked.

"Nothing anyone else wouldn't do. A lot of that goes on. We've kept in touch ever since Drockden went civilian," Grayson added.

"So, you and Drockden are friends. You sure don't act like it," Sandy said.

"Exactly. Something's wrong. When Drockden first arrived with Mark, I was doing an inspection. Drocken talked a lot and complained horribly, which he never does either of those. He's pretty shy. He even said the stewardesses were ugly. He would never make a comment like that. And he acted as if he'd never seen me before. That's not like Drockden at all," Grayson explained.

"Maybe he didn't recognize you," Carol suggested.

"I just saw him two years ago," Grayson answered and shook his head. "And for years, he's greeted me with the safety net same phrase. *'Hey, man, glad to meet you. I've heard you're a great guy.'* A code and safe greeting no matter who's around. He didn't say it this time."

Carol and Sandy listened intently. They waited quietly for Grayson to continue.

"Then, at the hotel, he offered you his arm," Grayson said, looking at Sandy. "Drockden would never do that. He's very timid with women."

"Maybe he's just changed," Carol suggested.

"Nah. This man looks like Drockden but can't be. The eyes are wrong and the mouth," Grayson said, and Sandy leaned in closer as he continued. "The last Christmas card that I sent Drockden, whenever it was, last year or two years ago, was returned. I assumed he'd moved with no forwarding address. I figured I'd hear from him later, but I never have."

"Have other people noticed anything?" Carol asked.

"With his career, he goes years without seeing his family."

Grayson paused. "Although, I checked the bank records and his mother still gets her automatic monthly deposit from him."

"Maybe Drockden has amnesia," Sandy said.

"I don't think so. As I said, he doesn't look right. Then I realized that if Drockden hadn't ignored me, I might never have noticed the facial differences," Grayson admitted. He stood up and paced. Sandy watched his every move.

Grayson continued. "It would be easy to take over Drockden's life. He keeps to himself. And by traveling so much, he makes acquaintances, not friends."

Grayson stopped and looked earnestly at Carol and Sandy. "Only one thing could mess up such a plan."

"What?" Carol asked intently.

"Our friendship. Most people don't know about it," Grayson said.

"Why?" Sandy asked.

"Because of Drockden's military reporting. We don't want people thinking I'm feeding him info," Grayson said and sat down. "Even though I'd never do that, people frequently make wrong assumptions."

"So, you were trying to get Drockden's fingerprints from Sandy's dirty dishes?" Carol asked.

"Yes," Grayson replied.

"That's no good. They didn't eat or drink here," Sandy said. "We got everything at the golf course and the restaurant."

"Uh, sorry to hear that," Grayson said and leaned back.

"I don't get it. Why would someone want to take over your friend's life?" Carol inquired.

"The why is easy. Drockden's welcome all over the world. Now, this imposter can go places most people could never access." Grayson paused and leaned forward. "The real question is, what is he doing here?"

They sat in silence, each of them deep in thought.

Grayson gave a deep sigh of concern. "I said National Security's at risk, but in reality, it's International Security in jeopardy!"

Chapter Eight

INGENUITY AND COURAGE

When it got late enough and very dark, Drockden exited the hotel and went into the desert for hours. It was still dark as Drockden returned to the hotel. He tiptoed and stopped at the front. He slowly scanned the area with a sinister smile before entering.

Drockden peeked in to see that the hallway was clear. He silently went to his room.

***

Arseneault and Carson were working in the aircraft hangar that morning. Carson was confused.

"What did Colonel Ortega mean about the regular wind sand problems aircraft face?" Carson asked.

"I know you're in training, so listen up. Ortega was talking about the necessity of a temperature-resistant, thermal-barrier coating," Arseneault replied.

Carson put up his hand and grinned. "In English, man."

Arseneault laughed and nodded. He demonstrated by spreading and closing his fingers.

"Metal expands when it gets hot. Jet engine blades get hundreds of degrees hot," Arseneault explained.

Carson nodded his head and intently listened. Arseneault covered his expanded fingers with his other hand. The two hands expanded and contracted together.

"The turbine blades are made with a special protective coating that's designed to expand and contract when it needs to," Arseneault explained.

"Like an accordion?" Carson said.

"Yes. These blades get so hot that when sand hits them, the sand turns to liquid glass," Arseneault said.

"No way. Seriously?" Carson asked.

"Yeah. And liquid glass will tear up almost anything. Think of molten volcanic lava. But that's not the worst," Arseneault said.

Carson was enthralled. "No wonder you love this stuff. It's cool."

"Got it—cool. That's where the real problem comes in," Arseneault explained.

"What?" Carson was bewildered.

"When the liquid glass starts to cool, it turns into a hard glaze over top of that protective coat. And that glaze won't move," Arseneault continued, and Carson's mouth opened wide. "The next time the jet goes up, and the blades get hot, that glaze won't let the thermal barrier—that protective coat—move like it needs to."

Arseneault returned to his hand demonstration. He held one hand stationary over the other so his finger could not fan open.

"They're working on ways to crack or melt the glaze off without damaging the protective coating, but it's not solved yet. It's a problem," Arseneault explained.

"Wow!" Carson responded.

"But that has nothing to do with our new sand problem," Arseneault said.

"You should be a professor," Carson declared.

Arseneault patted the plane. "You gotta be kiddin'. Why would I ever trade this baby for a paper airplane?" he asked, in all sincerity.

***

The hotel hallway was empty. Mark knocked relentlessly on Drockden's hotel room door.

"Come on, Drockden. Wake up. I have good news," Mark said.

Drockden sleepily opened the door, and Mark entered.

"Did you keep ringing the phone?" Drockden asked.

"Of course," Mark responded.

"Jerk," Drockden growled.

"You sleep more than any person I know. And no offense, but with all that shut-eye, you should look much better than you do. Maybe you need vitamins or something," Mark suggested.

"Thank you, Dr. Mark. I'll take two aspirin and hope you don't call me in the morning," Drockden replied.

"Sor-ry," Mark said sarcastically and flopped into the overstuffed chair.

"So. What's the good news?" Drockden asked.

Mark got excited. "We're invited to the golf course driving range."

"Sandy and Carol?" Drockden asked.

Mark grabbed a shirt and threw it to Drockden. "Who else? Get dressed. We can stake out the airport tomorrow. Besides, I'm paying a guy who works there to keep watch for us. He'll text me immediately if anyone famous or important shows up," Mark said.

"Ooooo. Smart," Drockden replied.

***

It was another sunny, hot day, which was getting a bit tiresome. Sandy and Carol were waiting at the bus stop and would have loved a few raindrops.

Sandy paced. "A year ago, I'd never been off the east coast, and now I'm halfway around the world trying to trap an international imposter. Go figure," she said with both hands extended and her mouth agape.

"This is not a soap opera. It's serious. Are you sure Mark and Drockden will meet us?" Carol asked.

"Mark promised. But we have to wipe off the golf clubs before we get with them. We've got to get these fingerprints," Sandy said.

"I see the air conditioning coming at last," Carol said gleefully as the bus turned the corner.

***

Grayson stood in front of a tent in the military area, watching the soldiers do maneuvers. Colonel Ortega drove up in a jeep.

"Got a minute?" Ortega asked.

"Sure," Grayson answered.

"Get in. I want your opinion," Ortega said. Grayson got into the jeep, and they drove off toward the airfield.

"This new sand problem we discussed is getting worse. Just in case there is some kind of sabotage involved, we've tripled the guard duty around the base's perimeter," Ortega said.

"That's good. We can't be too careful. Where are we going?" Grayson asked.

"I want you to see what the guys at the airfield have cooked up. I think it's pretty creative," Ortega replied.

They arrived at the airfield. Ortega smiled as he and Grayson exited the jeep.

"Hey, Arseneault, show the Lt. Colonel what you came up with to save your beloved planes," Ortega said.

Arseneault saluted. "Yes, sir."

He returned the salute. Ortega laughed and jabbed Grayson with his elbow.

"I think this guy used a propeller for a pacifier. I've never seen anyone love aircraft as much as he does," Ortega said with a huge grin.

Arseneault and Carson retrieved a hand-drawn poster with mounds of sand and dollar bills that said "Project Sand Dollar."

"Lt. Colonel Grayson, sir." Arseneault snapped to attention and saluted.

Grayson returned the salute and said, "At ease, son. 'Project Sand Dollar.' What is it?"

"Please look at this, sir," Arseneault asked.

"Lead on," Grayson motioned.

Grayson and Ortega followed Arseneault to the closest Blackhawk helicopter.

"For some reason, sand's ending up in the airflow box or the engine intake. Now, it's a constant problem," Arseneault said.

Arseneault pulled handfuls of sand from the helicopter intake and sifted it through his fingers to the ground. Grayson looked surprised.

"And can be deadly," Grayson said with concern.

"We keep trying to solve it but haven't," Arseneault responded in frustration.

Ortega nodded his head and gave an approving smile.

"So, I got this idea for a contest. We'll collect money. Half goes to whoever solves the sand problem and half to the charity for families of fallen service members, sir," Arseneault explained.

"Very resourceful plan. I like it. Double-check with the audit and regulations department. If there's no problem there, it sounds good to me. Great job," Grayson said and patted Arseneault on the back.

"Hot dog, sir," Arseneault responded excitedly. "With all this American ingenuity around here, I just know we'll solve this."

"I'm sure you will," Grayson replied with a big smile.

Grayson and Ortega turned to leave. Ortega turned back.

"Hey, Arseneault," Ortega said.

Arseneault turned and saluted. "Yes, sir."

"At ease," Ortega responds. "I just wanted you to know that there's a new zirconia coating that is going to be fantastic. Someday this sand will actually *help us*. Innovation usually means progress," Ortega said.

"Great news, sir," Arseneault replied. "These babies need to fly unharmed."

Chapter Nine

STRATAGEM PERSONIFIED

Carol was inside the golf shop next to the golf course on the compound. Sandy was keeping the manager busy outside. She had asked for help with her golfing strokes. Carol thoroughly wiped off all the golf clubs in two of the bags as Grayson had instructed her and carefully returned them to the golf bags. She then wiped off the two golf bags, as well. When Carol finished, she opened the shop door.

"Are you ready? We're late," Carol called.

Sandy and the manager entered the shop. Sandy winked at Carol.

"The golf cart's here and ready to go," Sandy said.

The manager picked up the two front golf bags. "I'll load these for you," he said.

"I've got this one," Carol said, carrying one of the cleaned golf bags with her towel and handing Sandy a towel, as well.

Sandy gently took the last golf bag of the four they had rented. All three exited the shop and went to the golf cart waiting outside.

"Do they have the balls at the range?" Sandy asked.

"Yeah, lots of them. Baskets and baskets," the manager replied.

They placed the golf bags in the cart, with Carol taking extra caution with hers. Sandy and Carol got in the cart.

"Thanks for the putting advice," Sandy said.

"Any time," the manager replied.

"Bye," Sandy said and drove toward the range.

"Drockden gets the bag with the small rip on the handle. That's the most important one. I think it will be easier to keep track of and not get mixed up. Mark gets the one you carried. We're sure to get fingerprints somewhere on the clubs or the bag," Carol said.

"I hope this works," Sandy replied.

"Me, too," Carol agreed.

As they arrived at the specified meeting area next to the driving range, they saw that Mark and Drockden were waiting. Sandy parked the cart, and she and Carol joined them. Sandy's purse was lying on the golf cart seat.

"Been here long?" Sandy asked, smiling.

"Just long enough to think we were at the wrong place," Mark responded with a grin.

"Glad you could join us," Carol said.

"You ladies must feel safe with all that security stuff at the gate," Mark commented. "Although, it was much easier to get in today since we submitted our life history to get approved. I think it was easier getting into Buckingham Palace than this place." Mark chuckled.

"We do feel very safe on the compound," Carol remarked. "They take security very seriously everywhere in the country but especially around here."

Some people walked by on their way to the driving range. Mark looked at the golf cart with an expression of concern.

"Your purse," Mark said and pointed.

"It's fine," Sandy answered.

Carol nodded. "Even though women's rights have a way to go in this region, there's very little theft here."

"Yeah," Sandy said. "If you get caught stealing, they cut off part of your finger. If you get caught stealing again, they cut off your hand." Sandy made a chopping gesture with her right hand to her left wrist.

"Whoa. That sure makes punishment swift," Drockden observed.

Mark looked confused. "I thought they cut off whatever it took to carry the stolen object. One hand versus two hands, or two hands and an arm depending on how big and how heavy the taken item is."

"Well, whatever. Somebody's cutting off something," Sandy motioned to Carol. "Like she said, very little theft."

"And less prison overcrowding," Drockden added. "We should implement some of this in the States. It sure would—"

Sandy cut him off. "Oh, no. Don't get Carol started on victims' rights and how being too lenient on criminals makes them commit more crimes. We'll be here forever." Sandy motioned to Drockden and Mark. "Let's grab some clubs, and we'll run for it," she laughed.

"I'm right there with you," Drockden responded.

Sandy maneuvered the bags so that Drockden took the one with the small rip on the handle, as Carol had planned. So far, the strategy seemed to be working. Sandy got her purse from the golf cart seat, and they walked onto the driving range.

The four of them practiced every stroke the girls could remember. Then Carol saw a guy with a chart listing the different strokes with illustrations. She found out she could get a chart from the counter inside the driving range shop. That helped them all tremendously. Carol and Sandy kept getting everybody to try different clubs so there would be a good selection of prints.

When they finished practicing at the driving range, they played nine holes of golf. That was all the heat Carol and Sandy could take for the day. Plus, Sandy had plans to meet Grayson with the clubs at the golf shop. The girls would be cooking dinner for Mark and Drockden at Carol's apartment, giving Grayson some safe snooping time.

Sandy sat in the golf cart, poised to leave, while Mark, Carol, and Drockden stood next to it.

"That was fun, guys," Sandy said.

"Yeah, till the wind got so bad," Drockden complained.

"True, but it was still fun," Sandy said. "I've got to go by the hospital to sign some forms. I won't be long. I'll meet you all at Carol's apartment. It's bigger and much nicer than mine."

"Aw, your place is nice," Mark said sweetly. "And we'd be happy to return the cart and clubs," he offered, looking into Sandy's eyes.

"No," Carol shook her head. "She checked out the cart, so she has to return it. They are stricter with the carts than the clubs."

"But thanks for the offer," Sandy smiled. "See you soon."

Sandy drove off waving. They all waved back.

"Bye," Drockden called, and Mark gave him a dirty glance.

Carol looked at the guys. "I would say, let's race to the bus stop, but at this temperature, it would be a race to the emergency room," Carol declared.

"I don't know how the troops stand to do maneuvers in this heat," Marked remarked. "It gives 'survival of the fittest' a whole new dimension."

"Yeah. If I didn't live and work in air conditioning, I'd have left the first week I got here," Carol admitted.

Mark laughed. "I agree. Oh, and the guards easily let us on the compound this time and didn't even require an escort. Just your phone verification. But not our car. We had to park it outside the gate. They said we could take the bus system anywhere we needed to go on the grounds. The visitor's passes work for all transportation points. Although, we still have to be off the compound by seven o'clock tonight. Our international reporter status got approved. It's handy to have and gets us into many places."

"I bet," Carol responded. "All over the world, huh?"

***

Sandy saw Grayson's jeep when she arrived at the golf shop. She hoped he had not been waiting long. Entering the shop, she saw Grayson browsing and joined him.

"Success, I do believe," Sandy declared.

"Did he suspect anything?" Grayson asked.

"Nothing," Sandy reassured him.

The manager walked over to them. "May I help you?" he asked.

"I'm just returning my cart and two of the golf bags. The other two will be returned later," Sandy said. "And thanks again for the tips earlier. They helped."

"Any time," the manager replied. "And you can keep the bags, but if they don't come back until tomorrow, it will cost you another day's rental for each of them."

"Not a problem," Sandy reassured the manager.

Sandy, Grayson, and the manager went to the cart. Sandy pointed to two of the golf bags.

"I want to keep these two," Sandy said.

"I'll get them," Grayson offered. He carefully picked one up and carried the golf bag by the bottom.

The manager had Sandy sign some paperwork while Grayson placed the golf bag gingerly in his jeep. When Grayson returned, Sandy pointed to the second bag she wanted him to take. Sandy thanked the manager and joined Grayson.

"We were very careful," Sandy nodded.

"Thank you for doing this. Want a ride?" Grayson asked.

"Please. It would sure beat walking to the bus stop in this heat," Sandy replied, getting into the jeep. "I handed Drockden the driver just the way you showed me. I think that's a good set of prints."

"I hope so. We need to know who this guy is," Grayson said.

"I'm one hundred percent certain the bag with the rip is Drockden's. And ninety-nine percent sure the other one is Mark's. If these prints are no good, we'll get some on Carol's water glasses when they're at her apartment," Sandy eagerly replied.

Grayson got in the jeep. "I appreciate you ladies helping. It's important. Truthfully, it's crucial. How long do you think I'll have to search Drockden's room?" he asked.

"At least three hours. We're cooking at Carol's instead of eating out so we can talk freely," Sandy explained as Grayson started the jeep. "And we'll probably play some games."

"Good thinking. It may be our only opportunity to do a room search," Grayson said.

"Mark and Drockden have to leave the compound by seven tonight, and they had to park their car outside the gate. Just keep that in mind," Sandy warned.

***

Sergeant Patrick Grimes entered Colonel Ortega's tent and took off his headphone set.

"A Saudi police chopper crashed," Grimes said.

"Why?" Ortega asked.

"They don't know yet, but they said they've been having terrible trouble with sand lately, too," Grimes replied.

***

Carol, Mark, and Drockden walked down the hallway to Carol's apartment. They were laughing and enthusiastic.

"Well, fellas, as they say, 'Welcome to my humble abode,'" Carol chuckled. She opened the door and invited them in with a sweeping arm motion.

Mark immediately started touching vases, statues, and artwork as they entered the apartment. Carol had some exquisite items in her home she had acquired while traveling.

"Wow! Waterford crystal, hand-carved olive wood, carved stone boxes from Serrano, Italy, I bet, chiseled marble artwork. You've got taste," Mark said admiringly.

"Well, thank you. Coming home to a nice place is important. And the longer I'm here, the more important it is," Carol said.

"I can understand that. Even though parts of this area are beautiful, I bet the boredom gets to you," Mark replied.

"That's true," she said.

"It can't be that bad. Millions of people live their entire lives here," Drockden said with some hostility.

"But they don't know what they're missing. Especially snow," Carol replied with a smile, and Mark laughed.

"Hey, wait," Drockden said. "It does snow here. Turaif, Tabuk, Arar, Shaqraa, and other places. It's just not as well known."

"I never knew that," Carol admitted.

"Me either," Mark added.

Drockden looked at his watch. "Can I use your restroom?"

"Of course. It's down the hall on the right," Carol answered.

Mark put his hand on his chest. "Well, I'm a huge fan of all the seasons. I could never live in California or Florida. I need to see the leaves turn gorgeous colors before they get brown, crackle, and die. And I like seeing all the new shoots of life in the spring—bright green blades of grass and new flowers poking through the ground. It would get boring to me if things never changed."

Then suddenly, Mark switched subjects. "So, how good of a cook are you?" he asked. "I'm starved."

***

Grayson watched both directions of the hotel hallway as he used an electronic lock pick and opened the door to Drockden's room. He entered the room quietly and closed the door.

Very carefully, Grayson tried to remove the decorative posts from the bed. He checked the drawers for false bottoms. Grayson searched every inch of the bedding and carefully checked between the mattress and the box springs. Then he went under the bed on his back with a flashlight and examined every possible spot where something could be hidden. Next, he lifted each leg of the bed, dresser, nightstand, and desk, thoroughly checking each one.

***

Colonel Ortega was reading in his tent. Private Ronnie Colms entered.

"Sir." He saluted.

"At ease, soldier," Ortega said.

"Look at the T-shirt I got for my mom. 'AMERICA'S not perfect, but it sure is THE BEST!'" Colms said.

"Where'd you find that?" Ortega asked.

"Two units over. They're selling like hot cakes. The proceeds go to Families of our Fallen Heroes. Want me to get you one?" Colms asked.

"I want three," Ortega replied.

Sergeant Grimes ran into Ortega's tent.

"Sir, a chopper's down," Grimes said in a panic.

Ortega stood immediately. "Let's go!" he said and rushed out of the exit.

***

Grayson lifted the carpet in the closet and examined the flooring. He sat and sighed. Grayson took his recorder from his pocket.

"I've looked everywhere. The only thing I've learned is that Drockden's addicted to popcorn, and housekeeping stinks. Popcorn's everywhere," Grayson recorded.

Grayson paused and scratched his head. He started recording again. "I'm going to Mark's room. If he's truly Mark, that is."

***

Carol, Mark, Drockden, and Sandy were seated at the table in Carol's dining room with empty plates.

"This is the best meal I've had since I got here," Mark said.

"Yes. Very good," Drockden added.

"We still have dessert," Sandy said.

"I have to wait for that. I'm stuffed," Mark admitted.

"Me, too," Carol replied.

"Well, it's warm homemade apple crumb pie with 'made from scratch' whipped cream," Sandy described and tempted everyone.

"Very shortly," Carol suggested and discretely kept an eye on Drockden. He looked at his watch.

"Please, excuse me. I need to use the facilities," Drockden said as he stood.

"Sure," Carol replied.

Drockden left, and Carol gave Sandy a look of suspicion. Carol looked at her watch.

***

Grayson was in Mark's hotel room, sitting on the floor. His head was leaning against the wall, and he started recording.

"I've found nothing in Mark's room either. Not even popcorn. But this Drockden's up to something. I just know it!"

Chapter Ten

RACE FOR TRUTH

Grayson entered James's office without knocking and found him plotting maps on the table. James looked up, nodded a nonchalant greeting, then went back to work.

"What? You've added a cot in here?" Grayson commented.

"Yeah. It's just easier for now," James admitted.

"Well, we finally got some fingerprints. They're running now," Grayson said.

"Great," James responded.

"This guy drives to the perimeter of the oil fields, just outside the military line," Grayson described.

"What's he doing when he's there?" James asked.

Grayson closed the door and walked closer to James. "He parks, walks into the desert, and disappears in the dunes."

"What about the oil field surveillance footage?" James suggested.

"He never gets that close. It's like he knows the range of the cameras," Grayson answered.

"That wouldn't be hard to learn." James accented his point with a motion of his hand that knocked a rolled-up map onto the floor. He quickly picked it up.

"Sometimes, he goes into the desert behind the hotel, too. I've even wondered if he was hiding drugs."

"That would answer some stuff. But there's still remote intel chatter about something big and bad coming."

"Not good. I can never get close enough to see without being spotted. I wish you could go with me to be my lookout."

"No time soon." James shook his head. "Not till the radio trainees get better."

"Then, yesterday, this came in the mail." Grayson took an envelope from his pocket and pulled out the pages from inside.

"Three pages with no fingerprints. The front and back pages are blank. The middle one says, 'Trust no one. The military operation is infiltrated.' Good thing I've known you since you were five." Grayson showed the typed page to James.

"Whoa! That is big," James said, his mouth ajar.

"It's addressed to me. There's no return address, and it's postmarked from Switzerland. I have no idea who sent this," Grayson said with a big sigh. "I even tried getting DNA off the seal of the envelope. But whoever is being this careful would also be smart about wetting the envelope seal."

"You'd better *be careful*. This changes everything," James warned.

Grayson put the pages back in the envelope. He took a flash drive out of his pocket and held up both items so James could see them.

"I will. But just in case, here's a copy of my audio journal on Drockden and this warning. And remember to avoid your cell. They're too easy to hack and trace. Only use our secure phones," Grayson said as he handed James the thumb drive and envelope.

"Oh, man. I better never need these!" James exclaimed, with panic rushing through his entire body.

***

Grayson hesitantly knocked on the door with the name-plate, "Chaplain Stallings." The chaplain opened the door quickly.

"Grayson! Great to see you. Come on in," Chaplain Stallings said excitedly. He took Grayson by the arm and guided him into the office, then shook his hand with genuine affection. "How are you doing?"

When Grayson didn't reply, Chaplain Stallings noted the trepidation on Grayson's face.

"Sit down," the chaplain said, pointing to a chair. His smile faded, replaced by a frown of concern. He could see something definitely was wrong. "What's up?"

They both sat down. Grayson hardly knew what to say. He looked directly at the chaplain. "I'm not even sure where to start," Grayson admitted. "And frankly, I'm a bit beside myself, as they say. Something bad is happening, and I don't know who to trust! And I'm considering asking for help from some unlikely sources. These are desperate circumstances."

"Well, you've got good instincts that you should follow," the chaplain declared. "I think it's a great sign that you are even considering asking for help. You try to shoulder way too much all by yourself. I know you've heard people say that 'God helps those who help themselves.' Well, I'm telling you that God helps those who aren't afraid to ask for help or who aren't too stubborn or too arrogant to ask for help even more! He wants us to reach out to one another. Opening up is hard. Developing trust takes strength and courage—especially with what you've been through."

***

When Mark and Drockden left to make their deadline for exiting the compound, the girls moved to Sandy's apartment. Grayson was coming there. It was night, and they were concerned because he had not yet arrived. Carol sat while Sandy paced.

"Grayson's two hours late. I just know he got caught, and Drockden's doing something awful to him," Sandy said. She stopped and shivered. "Drockden gives me the creeps. I hate the way he stares right through you. It's not natural."

"Grayson's too savvy to bungle a simple room search. He'll be here," Carol reassured Sandy.

"I wonder if he took the golf clubs back. Remind me to ask him, will ya?" Sandy said.

"You sure transferred that chunk of worry quickly, eh?" Carol laughed.

There was a knock at the door. Sandy was startled.

"Do you think that's him?" Sandy asked.

"Probably. Answer it," Carol directed.

Sandy opened the door, and Grayson was there with a small duffel bag. She pulled him into the apartment by his sleeve.

"Where've you been? We've been worried sick," Sandy fussed.

"She's been worried," Carol clarified.

"Well, we didn't know what happened to you," Sandy said.

"Please calm down. I just got held up at a briefing. See why I've never married," Grayson blurted out.

"Wait till you hear what Carol surmised about Drockden," Sandy paused. Then she added, "You've never been married? Do you have a girlfriend or fiancée?"

"No," Grayson said and turned to Carol. "What have you learned? I hope it's more than I got."

"Did you ever have a girlfriend or fiancée?" Sandy persisted.

Grayson was uncomfortable. He didn't want to answer but searched for a reply, knowing Sandy would not let this go. Regretting his comment, he put up his hand in a stop motion.

"That was many years ago," Grayson admitted. "Carol, what about Drockden?"

Carol looked sympathetically at Grayson. "It's just a hunch," she said. "I think Drockden's Muslim."

"Why?" Grayson asked.

"Either that, or he's got an incredibly regulated bladder," Carol replied.

"What are you talking about?" Grayson asked.

"One of the pillars of Islam is praying five times a day, all the way to the ground and up, facing Mecca. They have prayer calls at work," Carol said as Grayson listened intently and gestured for Carol to continue. "Both days we've been with them, Drockden always goes to the bathroom at intervals that correspond to prayer times," she said.

"Couldn't that just be a coincidence?" Grayson asked.

"He looks at his watch before he goes, and looking at the time doesn't trigger a bathroom urge," Carol responded emphatically.

***

Mark was seated at the desk in his hotel room and doodling. He sighed deeply.

"Sandy, Sandy. What do you think of me?" Mark paused and sighed again.

***

Grayson rubbed his face. "If Drockden is Muslim, he's not one of the peaceful majority. He's one of the troublemakers."

"There's more." Sandy motioned to Carol. "Tell him,"

"His comments. He's pro-violence and condones terrorist bombings killing innocent people, including children!" Carol said forcefully.

"This is bad," Grayson responded.

"How were the fingerprints?" Sandy asked.

"Good. They're running now. I'm waiting for the results. When you're searching the entire world, it takes a bit. Plus, I have to do this quietly and discreetly," Grayson replied.

"I bet," Carol responded.

Grayson paused, then quietly inquired, "May I ask you ladies a personal question?"

"Of course," Carol said.

"Do either of you have any religious convictions?"

"We're both Christians," Sandy said, almost in a whisper.

"Although, that's something we can't talk much about here. We have to be extremely careful."

"And we can only meet in small groups. Never in a church per se," Carol added.

"Well, have you noticed anything changing in the world over the last few years?" Grayson inquired.

"Like what?" Carol asked.

Sandy nodded her head. "For sure, we see that things get worse every year. It especially stands out to us because of living here. I don't like certain things that go on in this area—especially the treatment of women. But, in general, they do a better job of keeping the Ten Commandments. They're enforced here."

Carol huffed and put her right hand on her hip. "I'm not sure how much it counts if you're made to be good instead of choosing to be good!" Carol paused. "But there are some good things here. And when I go home, things like honor and integrity are much harder to find. My brothers were Boy Scouts back when they were called Boy Scouts. Almost everybody used to have some principles, whether they were scouts or not back then. But not so much anymore. People brag about cheating and stealing and getting away with bad stuff. The Golden Rule isn't followed like it used to be. Instead of 'Do unto others as you would have them do unto you,' now it's 'do whatever you can get away with no matter who it hurts or how wrong it is, as long as you don't get caught.' And even getting caught, people get away with tons of bad stuff!"

"Is that what you mean, Grayson?" Sandy asked.

"Yes. Well said, Carol. That and much more. I used to be a pretty good Christian." Grayson admitted. "Then something happened in my mid-twenties that made me very mad! I was so hurt and angry that I ended up blaming God, even though He had nothing to do with it. It was not His fault at all, but I couldn't see that back then. I spent years away from the church and away from God. I never planned that; it just happened. Year after year passed. I just didn't think about it after a while.

"Then, about five years ago, a buddy of mine died and caused me to do some deep reflection. I finally stopped blaming God for everything, which I should never have done in the first place. I realized how wrong I had been. And dumb. I ultimately came to my senses and went back to church. Then, I started praying some again. Although I'm still a work in progress. I've got a long way to go."

Carol and Sandy listened intently, not wanting to interrupt. Grayson paused and started again.

"I talked to one of the chaplains I like a lot, and we had some great conversations. I could not believe how I had lost so many years. He pointed out some things I had never thought about and told me some things I never knew. He explained how time is our most valuable asset. He said that when rich people are dying, what they want most is more time. But they can never get it. It's not for sale. Time is a gift from God that we need to appreciate every day.

"Also, the chaplain told me that the Devil—Satan and his evil spirit followers who God cast down to earth are very real. He said they have had thousands of years of experience and practice leading and tricking humans into getting them to do what they want them to do—going away from God! That is their goal! He said most people don't make a conscious decision to do that. It just happens. And that's part of the plan.

"According to the chaplain, people rarely talk about what they're genuinely feeling, so it gets all bottled up inside and affects their every move without them even realizing it. The bad thing or things that happen end up controlling them, and they don't even know it. It works to destroy them. I know it sure did me!

"Since that time, I've become aware of and seen so much more evil everywhere than there used to be. At least, it seems that way to me. Like, there has always been some child sex trafficking in certain places. In my work, you know about some of the horrible things in the world. But now, there is child sex trafficking going on everywhere. And it's rampant, even in America. It's sickening. It seems like evil's on overdrive.

"The chaplain told me to read Revelation in the New Testament, chapter twelve, but I haven't had a chance yet. He said that's where God cast Satan and his evil spirit cohorts down to earth. They're here. Right here. Now!"

"Wait. I have my Bible," Carol said and hurried to Sandy's bedroom and retrieved the book. "I think you're right. I've read that. Sandy and I have some scripture study together when we can."

"She's teaching me a lot," Sandy said.

"Aaawww. Got it." Carol was excited and emphasized certain parts as she read. "I have some verses highlighted. This is Revelation Chapter 12, verses 7 through 9 'And there was a war in heaven: Michael and his angels fought against the dragon, and the dragon fought and his angels, And prevailed not; neither was their place found any more in heaven. And the great dragon was cast out, *that old serpent, called the Devil, and Satan, which deceiveth the whole world: he was cast out into the earth, and his angels were cast out with him.*

"Then Revelation 12:12 says, 'Therefore rejoice, ye heavens, and ye that dwell in them.'"

Carol's voice got louder. "'*Woe to the inhabiters of the earth and of the sea! for the devil is come down unto you, having great wrath, because he knoweth that he hath but a short time.*'

"Now Revelation 12:17, 'And the dragon was wroth with the woman, and went to *make war with the remnant of her seed, which keep the commandments of God, and have the testimony of Jesus Christ.*' This is the King James Version of the Bible, my favorite. I love all the 'thee's and 'thou's. I think they're cool, and they remind me to show reverence to God."

"Wow," Sandy said. "When you think about it, that's kind of scary. . . and creepy. Like *The Exorcist* kind of stuff." Sandy grimaced. "I had a youth director priest when I was a teen that drilled into us that the Devil and his evil spirit followers are after us every day. He said that evil has a plan and a backup plan to get each and every one of us. He said they just have to get us started down the wrong path, and we're hooked. He warned us never to take the first step so you can stay safe."

"That's a good motto," Carol added. "But it's hard to do. It takes a lot of prayer and caution. My youth pastor Corky said, 'Life is like a softball game, and we're on Jesus's team fighting Satan and his evil team.' He said, 'Satan doesn't just want you to strike out; he wants you to join their evil forces.'"

Grayson rubbed his head. "That's great advice, too. And a great analogy. I could have used some of that wisdom over a decade ago."

Carol pointed at Grayson. "And I think you're right; evil is pushing harder, and more people are succumbing. A lot of the big preachers are talking about us getting closer to the Second Coming," Carol said.

Grayson stood and started pacing. "Of course, evil and bad choices have been here since the Garden of Eden, Cain and Abel, etcetera. But when you look at what is happening, you can see what those preachers are talking about. The getting worse part has seeped in while we've all been busy with life. Or maybe purposely distracted so it could quietly overtake us!" Grayson sat down.

Carol opened her hands toward Grayson. "I know nobody but God knows when the Second Coming will happen. Not even the angels in Heaven know. But we can see the signs of the times. When I think about it, I've seen some strong Christian friends become complacent or even fall away. And now that we're talking about it, I need to make some changes myself. I'm not bad, just not doing all the good I used to."

"I understand how that can happen. I was one of the fallen-away ones," Grayson admitted. "It transpires before you comprehend it. If someone had told me, back when I was young and regularly going to church, that I would spend years not going to church—I never would have believed them. But this is the first time in my life that I'm not sure who can be trusted in a military operation. There's only one guy in this whole venture who I know I can trust here. There have always been wackos here and there throughout the years, but never anything like this. It's like evil has infiltrated everywhere." He paused, then finished by saying, "I guess I'm starting to sound pretty wacko myself. Huh?"

"Not at all. Everything you said makes sense to me," Sandy said.

"To me, too," Carol agreed. "And just for the record, Muslims claim to keep the Ten Commandments, but their 'Thou Shalt Not Lie' has a huge caveat. They can't lie to other Muslims. But it is perfectly acceptable to lie to the infidels. That's us and anybody else who isn't Muslim. My Grampa was huge on truth. He taught us you shouldn't lie to anyone, period. Not even to your dog. If you say you are taking him for a walk, you better take him for a walk."

"We should all be big on truth," Grayson added.

"I like that," Sandy declared, nodding her head.

"You girls, I mean ladies, are very astute. I thought I could trust you," Grayson declared.

"You can. But what does that mean?" Carol asked.

"Trouble!" Grayson said unequivocally. "Trouble that I need your help stopping. I've got a big problem that is moving pretty fast."

Grayson opened his duffel bag, pulled out two sets of fatigues, and threw a set each to Carol and Sandy.

"You two have just been drafted. For your help, that is. I need trustworthy lookouts while I follow Drockden. And you two are my best option," Grayson said.

"What?" Sandy asked in sheer surprise.

"It's safe, and I don't know who else I can trust. The one guy on base I can trust can't leave his station. To use your phrase, we need to find out what this son-of-a-biscuit-maker is up to!" Grayson declared.

Chapter Eleven

OH, NO!

Outside the hotel, darkness had fallen like a blanket sheltering the area. Grayson, Carol, and Sandy were in a covered jeep, parked inconspicuously, watching and waiting. Sandy and Carol were wearing the fatigues and caps Grayson brought them. They both had their hair pushed up into the hats.

Abruptly, a taxi pulled up to the hotel entrance. Drockden got out of the cab and entered the building. Carol picked up the night vision goggles to take a look.

"You can't see him even with these?" Carol asked.

"No. He ends up behind the dunes," Grayson said. "And even infrared goggles that pick up heat signatures do not see through dunes. I wish they did. Also, I've had to be careful with no lookout. I don't want him knowing we're on to him. That's the last thing we need."

Grayson turned to Sandy. "Remember, you stay in the jeep. Carol to the left, and I'm going right," he instructed.

"Got it," Sandy said.

"Don't forget to speak softly into the microphone; otherwise, we'll all go deaf. These things are powerful," Grayson warned. "Let's do it."

Carol and Grayson quietly exited the jeep. Sandy got behind the steering wheel.

Moving to the left, Carol found a good spot. It was very dark out everywhere. Sitting and waiting, Carol saw the incredible beauty of the desert night sky peppered with sparkling stars that almost seemed close enough to touch. It was breathtaking. For the first time, she better understood the nomadic lifestyle of the Bedouins. Until now, she had always found their choices hard to fathom. Carol was humbled.

Drockden silently made his way down the hall to his room inside the hotel. Sandy was fidgeting in the jeep.

"Grayson, do you think he'll come?" Sandy asked.

"Patience. He has every night I've been here," Grayson replied.

"Okay. Patience is something I have to work on. Hey! A guy's walking out of the hotel, dressed in a black robe. He's wearing some kind of head covering, too," Sandy said.

"Stay calm. Keep watching," Grayson instructed.

"He's walking down the steps and toward the desert," Sandy uttered.

The man walked calmly toward the desert. He stopped to adjust his head covering and started again.

"Where is he?" Grayson asked.

"He's headed almost directly between you and Carol," Sandy described.

"Carol, do you see him?" Grayson asked.

"No, nothing," Carol responded.

"Keep watching. We can't lose him," Grayson encouraged.

Carol was looking through her night vision goggles behind a tree. Just the desert showed, and then Drockden walked into the vision area of her goggles.

"Wait. I've got him. It is Drockden," Carol excitedly whispered.

"Stay with him," Grayson said.

Drockden walked at a slow but steady pace. He paused and wiped his brow.

"I've got him now, too," Grayson said.

Drockden went between two small dunes and disappeared. They couldn't believe they lost him so soon.

"He's gone." Grayson huffed in frustration.

"Maybe there's a cave or a tunnel," Carol suggested.

"Not in this sand," Grayson said emphatically.

Sandy was in the jeep making faces, trying not to talk. She did not want to interrupt but wanted to know what was happening.

"Well, he's gone. Where is he?" Carol asked.

"What's happening?" Sandy blurted out enthusiastically.

"Ssshh. Just wait. We lost Drockden," Carol replied.

"Do you want me to—"

Carol interrupted. "Wait a minute, Sandy. Grayson, look."

Drockden suddenly reappeared between two dunes. He walked forward again.

"He's back," Carol said quietly.

"I've got him now, too," Grayson added.

"I've got it," Sandy said excitedly. "He must have been praying."

"Not likely," Grayson insisted. "Final prayer call was two hours after sunset. It's way past that."

"Hey, I thought these goggles would look through stuff," Sandy said.

"No. Like we discussed earlier, they're not infrared, just night vision," Grayson explained again. "And like I said before, even infrared will not look through a dune. While I have look-outs, I'm going closer. Keep watching."

Carol was lying on her stomach on the sand. She pushed herself up slightly.

"I'm coming, too," Carol insisted.

"No. It's too dangerous. Stay put," Grayson said firmly.

"But..." Carol protested.

"Stay put." Grayson insisted.

Carol hit the ground with her hand. "I wish we hadn't promised to follow orders."

"Well, you did. Or you wouldn't be here," Grayson advised.

"All right," Carol huffed.

Sandy was sitting in the jeep laughing. She was trying very hard to be quiet.

"I don't like taking orders," Carol admitted.

"No, but you sure like giving them," Sandy chuckled.

"Sshhh-sh," Carol responded.

"Sorry," Sandy replied softly.

Carol was still lying on her stomach on the sand. She watched intently. "I hope Drockden's just out meditating or something," she suggested.

"What's he doing?" Sandy asked.

"Just walking, but he's slowing down now," Grayson replied.

"He must be crawling. He walks so slow anyway," Carol observed sarcastically.

"He stopped," Grayson said as he looked through his night vision goggles. "He's taking something from his robe. Looks like two pieces of wood or pipe. I can't tell for sure. Now he's twisting them together."

Drockden took the third piece from his robe and twisted it onto the others. He knelt.

"He's adding another piece and got on his knees," Grayson observed.

"What is it? A clarinet? Is he hypnotizing snakes?" Sandy asked. "We saw that done once."

"It's a pole or something. He's added a flat piece and laid something on the sand from his headpiece," Grayson described.

Drockden repositioned himself. He held the pole with both hands.

"He made a shovel. He's digging," Grayson declared.

"Do you think he killed someone, chopped them up, and is burying the pieces?" Sandy asked sincerely.

Carol sat up and shook her head. "Get real," she said.

"Well, people do that, you know. And he's creepy", Sandy grumbled.

Carol smiled and put the palm of her hand to her forehead. She giggled but covered her mouth to keep quiet.

"He measured the depth with the pole and buried something. Now he's walking again," Grayson said.

"Maybe drugs, like you said," Carol suggested.

"He's walking faster, and it looks like he's counting his steps. Now he's digging again," Grayson said.

"Well—" Sandy started, but Grayson interrupted.

"Oh, no! Heaven, help us!" Grayson replied in shock.

"What is it?" Carol asked.

"If it's what I think it is, we'd all better start praying. Take the jeep back to your car and go home. I'll come to Sandy's by morning," Grayson declared.

"We can't just leave," Carol said.

"Go. Now. I'll be hours. Remember your promise," Grayson reminded them.

"You can't leave us hanging like this. At least tell us what you think this guy's doing," Carol stated.

"If I'm right, and I pray I'm not, he's planting explosives. This whole place may be one big bomb!" Grayson replied.

Carol was shocked and placed her hand to her mouth as she gasped.

***

Carol was asleep on the couch in Sandy's living room. Sandy paced and then shook Carol.

"Wake up. It's morning. How can you sleep? Grayson's got to be here soon," Sandy said.

"How can you be so chipper?" Carol asked. "I'm exhausted!"

"I'm not chipper, just anxious. I want to know what Grayson found," Sandy admitted.

"Spare me," Carol responded.

"I've been thinking. I bet Grayson's fiancée died, and he'd promised to love her forever, so he hasn't dated since. Isn't that so romantic?" Sandy said.

"You woke me up for this? Get a grip. Although, that would explain his heartfelt statement about life being hard," Carol admitted.

"And his being angry with God," Sandy added. "I thought of something else too. I have younger cousins still in college, and I can't believe the garbage they are getting taught. And the stuff that's coming at them all the time. It's frightening. It wasn't that bad when we were in college," Sandy motioned back and forth to herself and Carol. "And that wasn't that long ago."

"Ooooo. That's true," Carol said.

"Hey, maybe you can answer something that has always puzzled me. I never could understand how Bible heroes fell, like David and Saul," Sandy admitted.

"They were heroes, but they were also human," Carol said. "That's why we all need forgiveness through Jesus. He died for our sins. *No one but Christ is perfect.* And the Bible is clear, we ALL fall short of the glory of God. I had a Sunday school teacher who also told us that Satan has a plan for each of us. The question is, are we going to 'fall' for it? He said that Satan is very patient. He doesn't care when he gets you, just that he does get you. He also said that Satan's only real power is the power we give him! We forget that Jesus is way more powerful than the Devil. And often, we even forget to ask for help. Trying to handle things by ourselves is rarely the best choice."

There was a knock at the door. Sandy panicked and started fixing her hair.

"He's here." Sandy raced to the door and brought Grayson inside. "Good morning."

"The good's debatable," Grayson responded.

Carol sat up and rested against the arm of the couch. She quietly watched the exchange between Sandy and Grayson.

"Sit down," Sandy said.

The decorative couch pillows were on the chairs, so Grayson sat on the couch. Carol got straight to the point.

"What did you find?" Carol asked.

"Fingerprint results. Mark is Mark, but Drockden is really Manuel Martinez. A sadistic killer in the Fuego Mexican Drug Cartel. Two years ago, his rank moved way up," Grayson said.

Sandy threw the pillows on the floor and sat in the chair. She listened intently.

Grayson continued. "My guess is someone saw a resemblance to the real Drockden, and with what all they can do with plastic surgery nowadays, they perfected the look. It helped with the complexion that Drockden's mother is from India. All that made a perfect opportunity."

Grayson paused and cleared his throat. "There's a good possibility my friend's dead. He was highly trained and even kept training and improving his skills after he left the military. They'd never get him alive."

"Oh, dear," Sandy said and touched Grayson's arm with genuine concern.

Grayson hesitated but continued. "The real Drockden is one of the people I call a 'Protector Patriot.' He fights for and protects our rights and freedom. He loves America and all the good it stands for. He works to keep politicians and their deals with other countries honest. It's sad how many people will sell their soul and sell out their country for money! He's a hero, preserving our freedom, our lives, and our nation, just like many of the people serving in the military and, in reality, countless civilians. The Founding Fathers recognized and validated our God-given freedoms, but it's up to people like the real Drockden and us to keep it! As the Founding Fathers warned us. Drockden's one hero I don't want to be gone." He cleared his throat, fighting back emotion.

Sandy and Carol sat quietly, not knowing what to say. The stillness was deafening.

Grayson broke the silence. "The real Drockden used the phrase 'for real' a lot. And this is 'for real.' I miss him. But, staying on task, back to the current situation," he said. "The head of this cartel is madly in love with Zahwah, one of the Saudi princesses. But all of his gifts and proposals have been rejected. They're planning huge trouble!"

"Whoa," Sandy said.

Grayson gave a stern look. "And he's not Muslim. He's just trying to make you think he is. It looks like whatever is planned, they will try blaming on the extremists. Three years ago, they attempted to kidnap Zahwah when she was in Paris."

"Are you serious? What happened?" Sandy asked.

"The French police saved her, but the bad guys escaped," Grayson replied.

"Ugh, the wedding festivities!" Sandy said in a panic.

"Yeah, that's probably when they plan to make their move," Grayson acknowledged.

"What's in the desert?" Carol asked.

"Dear old Manuel, aka Drockden, wasn't praying between those dunes. He buried this deep enough so the wind wouldn't uncover it." Grayson took a packet from his pocket and held it out so they could see it.

"But I don't know how he's getting it here. Smuggling, bribery, or both," Grayson said.

"What is it?" Carol asked.

"An explosive—a type of extremely lethal plastique called PBX, with a receiver attached," Grayson explained.

Sandy and Carol both looked concerned. Sandy started rubbing her forehead.

"What's PBX?" Carol asked.

"Polymer-Bonded Explosive," he said.

"That doesn't sound good," Carol responded.

"It's not," Grayson warned. "With these planted at the proper distances, a chain reaction could destroy this entire section of the country. And give them plenty of time and cover to pull off whatever they have planned."

Carol and Sandy looked at each other with absolute shock. They were stunned.

Chapter Twelve

THE MOMENT

Even though the sky was clear, a helicopter flew erratically over the desert near Riyadh and then suddenly exploded. Pieces showered to the ground.

**

Ortega surveyed the helicopter crash site with Sgt. Grimes. Suddenly, there was another explosion in the distant sky. Grimes rushed closer to Ortega.

"Sir, did you see that?" Grimes asked.

"Yes! And that was not sand," Ortega exclaimed emphatically.

**

Grayson was still at Sandy's apartment discussing the situation and options. Grayson was pacing and contemplating.

"One man working slowly but surely is perfect. Had I not known the real Drockden, I never would have noticed anything," Grayson said.

"Have you arrested him yet?" Carol asked.

"No, and we won't. We need to know the time frame of this operation," Grayson explained.

"How are you ever going to find out?" Sandy asked.

"There's only one hope of getting that info fast. That's where you two come in," Grayson said, looking at both women.

"Us?" Sandy and Carol asked simultaneously.

"Yes. I'm sorry about your involvement, but I need your help again. We need to know how long Drockden plans to be here," Grayson admitted.

"This is frightening. Explosives?" Sandy said, putting her hands on her cheeks.

"Don't panic," Carol instructed Sandy. "We've got to solve problems, not make more."

"Panic is what I do. You're the calm one," Sandy said.

"Take some deep breaths," Carol told Sandy and turned to Grayson. "Of course, we'll help. We'll do anything we can."

There was a knock at the door.

"Oh, that's probably Callie. She's always borrowing something," Sandy said as she rose to answer it.

Sandy opened the door. Grayson and Carol could see the fake Drockden standing there from the couch. To conceal his identity, Grayson grabbed Carol and passionately kissed her.

"Oh. Hi, Drockden," Sandy said.

"I'm looking for Mark. He's not answering his cell. Have you seen him?" Drockden asked. His eyebrows rose as he spotted the couple across the room. The kissing grew more passionate.

"No, we haven't." Sandy scowled as she watched her friend and Grayson kissing. Searching for something to say, she finally explained, "That's Carol's old fiancé. He's the only one who's been by. They haven't seen each other in years. Ever since she called off the wedding. He's trying to win her back." She paused a moment and smirked. "Either that or smother her."

"If you hear from Mark, tell him he has an urgent message from his magazine. They are trying to contact him immediately," Drockden said.

The kissing continued, and Sandy stepped into the hallway.

"I'll tell him if we see him. It's nice of you to try to find Mark," Sandy said.

"Well, thanks. I'll keep looking. They may have some information on someone famous flying into town. Bye," Drockden said as he walked away.

"You're welcome. Bye," Sandy replied as she turned back toward the apartment.

Even though Sandy closed the door and walked to the couch, Grayson and Carol continued kissing. Sandy noisily cleared her throat.

"He's gone," Sandy said rather loudly.

Grayson stopped kissing Carol but still held her. "Oh, he's gone?" Grayson said. He and Carol hesitantly let go.

Looking at Carol, Grayson said, "I, uh, hope you don't mind. He can't see me with you two."

"That was quick thinking," Carol replied.

"The bit about the fiancé was a nice touch, Sandy," Grayson added.

"Thanks," Sandy beamed.

"Sandy, go get Drockden," Carol suggested with urgency. Carol motioned her hand toward the door.

"What?" Sandy asked.

"Catch Drockden. Make some kind of plans for today. It's a great opportunity," Carol said.

"Perfect," Grayson agreed.

"What about work?" Sandy asked, somewhat confused.

"I'll take care of that," Carol reassured Sandy.

"Since Manuel/Drockden saw Carol with me, you'll have to be the one to use your womanly wiles on him. Do you mind?" Grayson asked.

Sandy mockingly did a little curtsy. "There's not much choice now, is there?" she said with a salute.

"Thanks." Grayson smiled and nodded his head approvingly.

"It has to be you anyway; Drockden and I have fought too much," Carol reminded them.

"I'll be back," Sandy said. She hurried through the hallway, down the steps, and ran across the sidewalk to the compound transit stop. "Hey, Drockden. Wait up," she called.

***

Grayson looked at Carol and then stood. "I'd better go. Drockden may return. I'll call you—to discuss the plan."

Carol stood and looked at Grayson with both longing and confusion.

"I'll—wait to hear from you," she said.

Grayson looked at Carol and almost kissed her again. Dormant feelings surfaced, and he stopped himself. They walked to the door.

"Tell Sandy that I have this place wired, so I'll hear every-thing," Grayson reassured Carol.

"You bugged Sandy's apartment? She's gonna love that," Carol replied.

"I hope she's not too mad," Grayson said.

"All things considered, I'm sure she'll understand." Carol smiled.

Grayson looked at Carol and paused. "I should leave," he said.

"Of course. Watch out for Drockden," Carol warned.

"I will. Bye." Grayson left the apartment and moved quickly down the hall.

"Bye," Carol called from the doorway, watching until he was gone.

Then she slowly closed the door. She leaned her head back against it. She started to walk, then turned back and leaned her head against the door again.

"Note to self: This just has to be the moment. Oh." Carol rushed to the phone and pushed four numbers. She listened while the phone rang on the other end; someone picked up. "Anna," she said, "I'll pay you twelve hundred dollars to work Sandy's shift. Does that work for you? Thanks."

Carol hung up the phone, paused, and smacked her palm on her forehead.

"For heaven's sake. Now I'm wondering about Grayson's dead fiancée.

Chapter Thirteen

SHOCK AND AWE!

At the temporary US Military Section, Colonel Lewis Harmen was talking to Grayson in the colonel's office. Grayson was desperately trying to exit.

"But sir, I was just leaving," Grayson said.

"This won't take long, and it's good public relations. This country music guy's here filming part of a video. He just wants to meet you," the colonel replied with a firm look.

"Okay, sir," Grayson reluctantly agreed.

The colonel smiled. "They should be here soon, and we'll be quick."

Abruptly, noises came from the hall. "I think that's them now," the colonel said excitedly as he moved to the door.

Colonel Harmen opened the door, and two guys entered. They were very respectful and appreciative of being there.

"Hi, I'm Frank, the singer, and this is John, my cameraman," Frank said, then extended his hand to the colonel. They shook hands.

Frank kept smiling. "Thank you for all your help. We're finished packing up at the hotel and flying out in three hours," he explained.

"We're delighted we could be of assistance. And this is Lt. Colonel Grayson, that you wanted to meet," Colonel Harmen said with his practiced charisma. Grayson's charm was natural.

Then Frank and Grayson shook hands. Grayson tried very hard not to seem impatient.

"It's nice to meet you. My cameraman's brother is a real fan of yours," Frank said and motioned to John.

"Is that right? I didn't even know it was possible for me to have a fan. Not many people know me. It's nice to meet you guys, too," Grayson said and shook the cameraman's hand.

"Hey, man, glad to meet you. I've heard you're a great guy," John said.

Grayson was stunned at that greeting and looked intensely at the cameraman, then stared into his eyes. Grayson was astonished. That was the greeting the real Drockden always gave him. He was not at all sure what to do. This man did not look like the real Drockden one bit.

John looked at Grayson. "I've got some camera equipment back at the hotel that my brother thinks you'd like to see if you want to stop by."

Initially, Grayson wanted to leave. However, with John's greeting, Grayson wanted to hear anything and everything John had to say. Nothing could keep him from going to their hotel room as soon as possible.

***

Grayson quickly entered the hotel and got in the elevator. He went to the ninth floor, rapidly walked to room 942 as instructed, and knocked. John, the cameraman, answered.

"Need any help packing up equipment?" Grayson asked.

"That'd be great. Come on in," John said.

Grayson entered but was still very confused.

"Frank's in the gift shop picking up some last-minute presents. He'll be awhile," John said. He closed the door and enthusiastically turned toward Grayson. "I thought you'd never get here. Did you get my letter from Switzerland?" John asked.

Standing in silence, Grayson studied John's face. He was not sure what to think. "What?" Grayson asked.

"It's me, Drockden!" John said vehemently.

"You don't look right at all," Grayson observed, looking utterly stunned.

"I've had my jaws and cheekbones broken and redone so that facial recognition won't get me," John said. "It's me. For real." He gestured to his face. "Electrolysis on my hairline. Real bone chin and cheek implants. And my face and hand skin bleached. I've been through hell. And ladies elect to get this stuff done. It's nuts."

Grayson just stared.

"Tripwire? The Marines? You saved my life!" John said, with both arms out.

"It is you!" Grayson grabbed Drockden, hugging him and picking him up. "It really is you," he said, fighting back tears of joy. "Thank goodness you're alive. I thought for sure you were a goner."

"For real, man," John responded. "I thought I was a goner, too. Still worried about that."

"Your phrase and eyes got me here, but I wasn't sure what was happening. Thought you had an unknown brother or something," Grayson admitted.

"I'm living in the twilight zone and trying to keep alive... with God's help. Boy, we take God for granted until we majorly need Him. At least I did. Keep calling me John. We can't slip up. I've got to fill you in as much as possible in case something happens to me," John said, pointing to the chairs.

They sat in chairs facing each other. Grayson couldn't believe Drockden was really alive. He was ecstatic and listened attentively.

"There's a guy who goes by Sam," John said. "He's mean and sadistic. And, in my book, very evil. But mega-rich and extremely powerful. He causes trouble all over the world just for fun. He's hurt many countries and killed countless people with no qualms whatsoever."

Grayson hung on his every word, absorbing it all intently.

John continued. "He's caused numerous bank failures, stock market plunges, oil problems, economy crashes. The list goes on. But now his goal is to start World War III, or something close to it."

Grayson was shocked. "How do you know him?" he asked.

"He hunted me down because of my connections, wanting me to help him. He offered me millions—said I could name my price, all the way up to a billion dollars. That's how he has gotten so many people working for him. The guy's unbelievably rich. I knew the only way to get out of it and protect my mom and sisters was to fake my death." John squeezed the arms of the chair.

With a deep sigh, John, the real Drockden, rubbed his neck with both hands and started again. "I escaped from him and his henchmen once at my hotel in DC by jumping out of the window. Then I used all my training skills to stay hidden, but they found me one night at George Washington University, where I guest teach sometimes. I was being chased again by three thugs in suits. I ran into the university. Man, I never prayed so hard in my life! Fortunately, those thugs were out of shape, exhausted, and breathless. So, they surrounded the building. I heard one yell, 'We'll wait till everybody leaves.'

"I went to the fitness center, avoiding the security cameras, and got my gym bag out of my locker. Then I entered the fitness center with my passkey. People were working out and clueless. A sweaty guy was going at it on a treadmill, and I discreetly took his keys from the floor next to his bag. I'd seen him come from the Baseball Athletic Department many times before.

"So, I went into the baseball room with his key and took two warm-up suits, two hats, and a pair of sneakers. Put them in my gym bag. Next, I went to the Dissection Clinic for the Medical Students. There were tables with covered cadavers in various stages of dissection. I surveyed the selection of whole bodies, pausing at a table holding severed heads. Very eerie. I checked all the complete bodies for height, size, and flexibility. Then finally chose one with no scars relating to a break and no signs of any broken bones—wearing surgical gloves, of course. I made sure to rearrange the whole cadavers so you could not tell one was missing.

"I dressed in a warm-up suit and hat, then dressed the corpse in the other warm-up suit, hat, and sneakers—which was disturbing. But I was desperate. I pulled his jacket collar up high, so his neck and head were almost covered. The hat took care of the rest. I put the cadaver's stiff arms around my neck, with the body on my back, and we made a quick detour to the skin graft teaching section. He was missing some chunks of skin. I filled a black trash bag with slabs of flesh and put him on my back again. I held his arms, the black trash bag, and my gym bag tight as I went down the steps.

"Very slowly, I opened the exit door slightly and looked around. I was petrified. I pushed the key fob, making the car lights flash, to identify and unlock the car with the keys I had taken. We, that is, the cadaver and me. By this time, I was calling the stiff Bruce to make him seem less creepy. Now, I'm walking with Bruce by my side, walking to look like Bruce was intoxicated. We carefully made our way to the car matching the stolen keys.

"Reaching the car, I placed the corpse across the front seat. Then I immediately pushed the interior light switch off. I pushed both front seats back, got in, closed the door, and went to work. I spread the slabs of skin all over Bruce where he needed them—you know, the skin that I had taken out of the skin graft teaching section refrigerators. That was very creepy, but he had to be all covered for the flesh to char convincingly. The bag of skin to fill his missing chunks was even more disgusting than Bruce.

"Next, I pushed the cadaver's hip joints and knees to a bending position. It was a struggle, and one hip joint broke with popping and crunching sounds. Scared me to death. Whew! After posing Bruce in the driver's seat, I buckled the seat belt and adjusted his hat and jacket collar. I stuck his hands on the big part of the steering wheel and put some of his fingers around the steering part. The entire time I was posing him, I had to readjust the loose slabs of skin! That was creepy too, but I had no time to think—just do! Even cutting the skin with the scissors from the lab was gross. I could never be a doctor. I got everything set in the car.

"There was a maintenance shed and some lawn equipment close by with lots of bushes for hiding. I picked the lock of the maintenance shed and looked around. I found a massive can of gas and a pair of pliers, which I took back to the car. I used the pliers to pull all of Bruce's teeth, putting each one in my zippered pocket. I should have done that before I positioned him. I had to redo a lot of what I had already done. I figured the missing teeth would make it look like torture—I couldn't take a chance on dental records being checked. I doused Bruce, making sure to soak the clothes and skin. I ripped Bruce's seat in several places and filled each cavity with gas. I saturated the car's entire interior with gasoline, including the carpet and the roof.

"I returned to the maintenance shed and picked up two more sizeable cans full of gas and eight large aerosol cans of bug spray. I surrounded Bruce with cans of bug spray. I quietly drenched the front exterior of the car, including underneath, and put more gas on the inside. Then I returned the empty gas cans, placed the nasty skin plastic bag in my gym bag hiding in the bush, and headed back to the main building.

"One of the suit thugs was sitting on the steps at the front entrance. So, I ran across the grass and ensured he recognized me. He whistled, and the chase was on. Staying considerably ahead, I led them to the back parking lot and the car containing Bruce. I opened the driver's door and dropped to the ground. Then I flashed the headlights, slammed the door, and scooted underneath the back of the car to the other side. I had to take off my jacket because it got gasoline on it. Luckily, I had on a black shirt underneath. Then, I threw a lit lighter from the maintenance shed into the partially opened front passenger car window and rolled under the SUV next to the car.

"Man, the fire raged. I screamed as loud as I could, hiding behind the nearest car. The thugs saw the fire and hat bill silhouette. They stopped running and watched, listening to my screams. Flames engulfed the interior and the whole front of the car. Then the bug spray cans began to explode.

"The thugs just stared with their mouths open. People started coming, and then the thugs immediately left. I ran in the opposite direction, grabbing my gym bag from the bush and holding my gasoline-soaked jacket away from my body, just in case. People came from everywhere. I heard sirens, but I didn't stop," John said with a deep exhale.

Grayson's eyes were wide. "Wow, Drockden, I mean John. You sure put your special training skills to good use. I'm so thankful you escaped. Great plan, buddy. Especially spur of the moment. Unbelievable! I'm impressed once again," he said, giving John another hug. He was genuinely grateful and amazed his friend was alive.

"I only made it with God's help. The cadaver and skin had to be charred beyond recognition for this to work and keep my family safe. It has been an absolute nightmare. Many times, I thought I was going to die." John took a deep breath and changed the subject. "Oh, a nose shortening, and my hair's colored," he admitted.

"I figured out those two. What can I do to help? My house is empty. You're welcome to live there," Grayson offered.

"I may take you up on that. It'd be nice to have a home base," John said.

"I don't have a key with me, so just break in any time," Grayson responded.

They both laughed.

"There are two trustworthy CIA agents I've known for years who have helped me. New identities, surgeons, everything. You three are the only ones who know what's happened," John confided.

"You're right, the Twilight Zone," Grayson agreed.

John rubbed his hands together. "They are unofficially working to find everything they can on Sam and what's planned because we don't know who can be trusted. Too many people have become sell-outs." John stood and paced. "Sam has people in high positions throughout the world. He's bought peoples' souls, and they are even selling out their families and their countries."

John took two cartons of milk from the refrigerator and handed one to Grayson. Grayson laughed, "So this is how you've never had a broken bone. I'm vowing to drink more milk." They chuckled.

John rubbed his chin and looked intently at Grayson. "This whole experience has me questioning almost everything. Now, every time I see a politician or a judge vote for or against something that's out of character or doesn't make sense, I wonder if they have been secretly replaced or threatened with harm to their family. The ramifications and possibilities of this are frightening. It is mammoth! And watching Sam and his operation, I've learned that power is more addictive than money or even the strongest drug out there! Holding onto that power becomes all-consuming—regardless of the cost to people or countries or even countless lives being taken. Trust no one," John warned.

John took a drink of his milk and continued. "For that matter, when I see news reporters skewing facts or situations, I wonder the same thing. Have they been replaced, threatened, or bought off? Oh, and never trust any form of wired or wireless communication. Only use secure lines that you've created."

Grayson pondered. "And they can't just take Sam out because someone would probably just take his place? It seems like that network must be intricately protected."

"Yeah," John agreed. "Some of his people are as evil as he is, although many are coerced. But finally, we may have two good guys on the inside. They can't get rid of Sam until they can decimate the entire operation!" John exclaimed urgently.

"One thing is for sure, this fake Drockden is bad news," Grayson emphatically responded.

John looked seriously at Grayson. "I need you to help stop him. The world needs you to help stop him. But we need to know his plans before he can be stopped. We think it begins here and—" John was interrupted by the door opening.

Frank entered, smiling and carrying lots of packages. "I got lots of good stuff. You should've come with me," Frank said.

***

A local man, Youssef, entered the temporary US Military section. He stopped in James's doorway.

"Good day, James. Do you want to buy another satellite dish?" Youssef said with a huge grin and a wave.

James looked up and smiled. "Hello, Youssef. Good to see you."

Youssef smiled. "I forgot to ask you. When I get the upgrade boxes for your dishes, do you wish me to bring them here?"

"What boxes, and when are they coming?" James inquired.

"The seller told me soon, and they're free. They are the newer higher-definition boxes," Youssef explained.

"Hmmm, interesting. Yes, please bring those here as soon as you get them," James requested.

"Oh, I will. You are a good customer. Have a great day," Youssef said as he exited.

"You, too," James responded.

After Youssef left, James quickly closed the door. He made a call on the secure phone.

"Grayson, it's James. It may be nothing, but I've got to talk to you asap in person. It's crucial. Stop by as soon as you can. I have new info...."

Chapter Fourteen

HOPE AND HORROR!

Mark, Drockden, and Carol were seated in Carol's living room. Sandy was running and doing a charade. Mark was desperately searching for the answer.

"Running. Row and running. The Roadrunner," Mark shouted.

"That's it," Sandy exclaimed.

"Good one," Carol said, putting the snack dishes on the tray. Sandy helped her.

"Mark, it's your turn to think of one to do. We'll be right back," Carol said.

Sandy and Carol carried dishes into the kitchen. Sandy jabbed Carol.

"I like Mark," Sandy admitted. "He's so sweet and thoughtful. And fun."

"Yeah, he is. And it's so hard to compete with a dead fiancée," Carol replied with a wink and a smile.

"We don't know if that happened," Sandy said.

"True. But we can't help but wonder what has happened," Carol admitted.

Mark joined them in the kitchen. "Hey, can we do something else? I can't think of a good charade."

"How about Scrabble?" Carol suggested.

"I don't know. I can write, but my spelling is atrocious. Just ask my editor," Mark admitted.

"We're all bad. We can play partners, so no one will know who's the worst. It'll be fun," Sandy said with a chuckle.

"Okay. Let's do it," Mark said as they headed back into the living room.

"Ooooo," Sandy was excited. "When we were sharing funny stories, I forgot about this one. When I was on vacation in the States, I met a guy at the beach. When he discovered I was a nurse, he told me he was a doctor in the Marine Corps. I was very impressed until I talked to Carol. She laughed so hard she couldn't breathe. Then Carol finally explained to me that there are no doctors or medical personnel in the Marines at all! Carol said the Navy handles any of the medical care that's needed for the Marines.

"Boy, did I feel stupid. But I couldn't just let it go. There was a great payback. We went to a dinner party at this guy's friend's house. That's when I announced that he was not a doctor or a Marine. He was so embarrassed he choked on his drink and almost turned purple. Not only was he a liar, but he was a pretty dumb liar. Only one guy knew he had told me that nonsense, and none of the girls. It felt so good to rat him out. And I got to knock him into the pool before I left in an Uber," Sandy said with much satisfaction. "I guess we all get suckered by scum sometimes."

They all laughed. Mark watched Sandy's every movement and was completely infatuated with her.

"That is pretty funny," Mark said. "But I must admit, I didn't know that the Marines have no medical personnel. Even with all my research. However, I did learn that there are only ever less than two-hundred-thousand active Marines at any one time."

"Really?" Sandy asked.

"Yep. That surprised me," Mark replied. "And they say, 'Once a Marine, always a Marine.' So, there technically are no former Marines, like they say about other military branches."

"I didn't know any of that," Drockden admitted.

"Oh, Drockden, we decided to switch to Scrabble," Sandy remembered. "The game's at my house. Want to go with me to get it?"

Drockden was happily astonished, and Mark was obviously disappointed. He watched Drockden for a response.

"Sure," Drockden quickly replied.

"While we're gone, you guys can cook," Sandy suggested.

"Good idea," Carol said as Sandy and Drockden left.

Mark was quiet and still. He did not move. Carol felt his frustration.

"Well, she couldn't leave Drockden with me. We'd kill each other," Carol said and laughed.

Mark laughed too. He got up and started helping Carol prepare the vegetables and marinate the steaks.

***

Grayson was on the compound, waiting at the back of Sandy's apartment building. There was no one else around that area. He was dressed in Arab attire and had an earpiece connected to Sandy's apartment bug. He quietly spoke into his recorder.

"I'll be able to hear everything that goes on in Sandy's apartment. I just hope Sandy can pull this off," he sighed.

***

Sandy opened the door to her apartment. She and Drockden entered.

"Here we are," Sandy said, placing her keys on the entry table.

"That was a farther walk than I expected," Drockden admitted.

"Yeah, you're right. I need to rest my feet before we head back," Sandy said as she took off her fancy shoes. She sat down on the couch, placing her legs under her in a relaxed position.

Drockden watched Sandy carefully and intently. Sandy forced herself to stay composed and not fall apart, although she was a bundle of nerves.

"This is the first chance we've had to talk. You're very cute," Sandy said and gave a cheesy smile.

Drockden looked puzzled but sat down on the couch next to Sandy. He was not sure how to respond. "Well, thank you. You are very cute yourself," he said.

"I bet women all over the world find you irresistible," Sandy said, trying to give a flirty look.

***

At the back of Sandy's apartment building, Grayson shook his head and started recording.

"This was a bad idea. Worst idea ever. Sandy sounds like a bad B-list movie. Why did I think this would work?"

***

A helicopter was out of control and struggled to land. It plummeted to the ground. GIs close by rushed around gathering equipment while Sgt. Stewart Belvue radioed for help. Everyone was in rescue mode.

"A chopper's down. Send medics immediately!" Belvue said sternly.

The medics arrived and flew into action. Fearing an explosion, GIs had already pulled some wounded soldiers from the crash. Their blood-soaked uniforms were frightening. GI Kyle Hoffman looked terrible, and they put him on a stretcher. Hoffman took a bloody picture from his pocket and handed it to a medic.

"Collins, take care of my kids if I don't make it. Please," Hoffman said. The medic, Andrew Collins, unsure of what to do, took the photo.

Soldiers sprayed the helicopter with foam and examined the wreckage. Colonel Ortega arrived in a jeep as a GI ran to meet him.

"Sir, there's so much sand in there; it's like someone poured it in," the GI said.

"I'm sure they did!" Colonel Ortega responded. "But who? Why wasn't this craft examined before take-off?" Ortega said gruffly.

"Sir, it was," the GI replied.

***

Drockden/Manuel, and Sandy were standing in her living room.

"Now you promise you'll come by tomorrow? If you're leaving in a week, that doesn't give us much time together," Sandy said, trying her best to be romantic.

"Wild camels couldn't stop me," Manuel, the Drockden impersonator, replied and grinned.

They both laughed.

"Good. I'm holding you to it," Sandy smiled as she picked up the Scrabble game and walked to the door.

"I guess we'd better get back, Manuel. Carol and Mark will..." Sandy hesitated as she realized her mistake. "...be wondering why we're so late."

Manuel stood and stared coldly at Sandy. She was terrified. Sandy never liked how he looked at people, and this was even worse.

"Let's go," Sandy said. She quickly opened the door and entered the hallway, not even caring about locking the apartment.

Sandy rushed down the hall. Manuel quickly followed her. He took a knife from his pocket that glistened in the light. Manuel promptly walked up to Sandy, placed the blade at her side, and squeezed her arm.

"How did you find out I was Manuel?" he asked.

"What do you mean? Manuel's my old boyfriend," Sandy said, her voice quivering.

"Nice try," Manuel replied in a sinister growl.

An apartment door down the hall opened. Manuel looked at Sandy.

"Walk if you want to see tomorrow," he snarled.

***

138

As he moved to the front of the building, Grayson frantically maneuvered as quickly as he could. He could not believe what he had just heard and desperately tried to get to Sandy.

***

Colonel Ortega was at the helicopter crash site giving orders to the GIs. "I want every piece of debris cataloged. Nothing flies until we get answers!"

Sgt. Grimes arrived in a jeep, and Ortega walked to Grimes. "Corporal Robinson died, sir," Grimes whispered.

Ortega's head drooped. "Will the rest make it?" he asked.

"They don't know yet, sir," Grimes replied with a panicked look and lowered his head.

***

Manuel and Sandy were now inside the utility room in the basement of the apartment building. The padlock was unlocked and simply hanging to Manuel's delight, making for easy entry. Sandy was lying on the floor, with Manuel on his knees beside her. Manuel had Sandy pinned down with his left arm pushing on her throat. Shelving with cleaning supplies lined the walls. There were mops and brooms in the corner. Manuel shoved a rag in Sandy's mouth and then put his knife to her face. Sandy was shaking uncontrollably.

"Don't make me cut your pretty little face, girl," Manuel said as he ran the back edge of his knife along Sandy's left jaw with his right hand.

Sandy was petrified and thought she might vomit at any moment. Her head was spinning and pounding.

"I want to know who found out about me and what they know," Manuel said brusquely. He grabbed Sandy's throat with his left hand and kept the blade at her face. "You better talk! Tell me what I need to know."

***

Mark and Carol were seated at the table they had set for dinner. Mark was talking, but Carol was preoccupied.

"...so, I said, 'Maybe she'll say yes,'" Mark laughed, but Carol did not respond. "Are you listening?" he asked.

"I'm sorry. I'm wondering where Sandy and Drockden are. They've been gone too long. The desserts are even getting cold," Carol replied with heartfelt concern.

"It has been a long time," Mark pondered. "Should we try her cell phone?"

"I guess we should wait a little longer," Carol said, unconvinced of her own words.

Suddenly, Carol's house telephone rang. It startled both of them.

"That's probably Sandy," Mark said, trying to reassure Carol as she grabbed the telephone.

"Hello. No. We haven't heard from Sandy," she responded.

Grayson was in Sandy's living room. He squeezed the telephone receiver. "I'll get back to you." He quickly hung up and rushed into the hallway.

Grayson continued banging on doors and yelled Sandy's name. "SANDY!"

***

Manuel and Sandy were still in the utility room. Sandy had stuck to her story that *Manuel* was her old boyfriend. She could see no reason to deviate from that, and she felt it would be worse if she did.

Manuel was not buying that story. He lifted her off the floor by her throat with his left hand. Manuel was enraged and strangled Sandy. Manuel stabbed her on her left side, and blood began to flow. "Tell me!" he growled viciously. He stabbed her again on the left side, trying to get her to talk. Sandy struggled to free herself and immediately gasped for air from the second stab wound. Sandy became limp and passed out. Manuel dropped her body back to the floor.

"You should have told me," Manuel barked. He picked up the knife he had dropped and bent down to Sandy. "No female tricks me. Die slow," he said.

Manuel made a shallow slit halfway across Sandy's throat. Blood trickled down her neck. Suddenly, Manuel heard Grayson faintly calling for Sandy. Manuel turned, looked at the door, and spilled the Scrabble game from the paint bucket onto the floor. He left quickly. Manuel quietly closed the utility room door and put the metal hasp back in position. Grayson was calling for Sandy again. Manuel placed the lock on and locked it. He looked again and fled immediately down the basement hallway, in the opposite direction of Grayson's voice.

Grayson still banged on doors and then ran down the stairs to the basement. Sandy was on the floor in the utility room with blood on her side and neck. Grayson continued to yell, "SANDY!"

Sandy began to stir and slowly awakened, though her breathing was labored. She heard Grayson calling. She was frail and pulled at the cloth in her mouth, but she did not have the strength to get it out of her mouth. Sandy tried to yell but could not. She saw the spilled Scrabble game. She pushed the box forward the best she could, which caused letters to go under the door.

Grayson spotted bloody Scrabble letters coming out from under the door. He rushed to the utility room door and banged. "SANDY!"

Two more letters came out from under the door. Sandy's arm collapsed to the floor as she struggled to breathe.

"I'm coming in," Grayson shouted.

Tears ran down Sandy's temples and into her hair. Grayson saw the lock, threw off the Arab clothing, and repeatedly kicked the lock area with his combat boots. The metal pulled away from the facing and then fell. He grabbed the doorknob to keep the door from hitting anything.

The door opened quickly but carefully, with him restraining it. Grayson rushed inside. He hesitated when he saw Sandy. Grayson could hardly believe his eyes.

"Oh, no! Sandy, I'm here. It's going to be okay," Grayson said. He wanted to sound reassuring, but he was horrified.

Grayson ripped off his shirt and tore it into pieces. He bandaged her neck. Then Grayson placed material at Sandy's side and applied pressure. Gently, he removed the gag from her mouth.

"You're gonna be all right. I'm getting you out of here," Grayson said, hoping he spoke the truth.

Tears rapidly flowed from Sandy's eyes as Grayson picked her up and ran out of the room. He dashed into the hall carrying Sandy and ran up the stairs.

"I'm so sorry you're hurt. I should never have gotten you into this," Grayson said as he ran.

Sandy struggled to speak and responded quietly. "I blew it, not you."

"You were wonderful," Grayson replied as he kept going.

"You don't have much time," Sandy said, struggling faintly.

"Shhh. I heard you say he's not leaving for a week. Save your strength," Grayson encouraged.

"But... back..." Sandy said and fell unconscious.

Grayson ran as fast as he could go. "Hold on." The whole time, he silently prayed, *God, please help us! Please don't let Sandy die.*

***

Mark was jittery. "What's taking so long? I'm going to Sandy's," he said. Mark headed to the door, and Carol panicked.

"Wait. We need to stay here. Drockden and Sandy should be back soon. As you said, it can't be much longer," Carol responded.

The phone rang.

Chapter Fifteen

THE SUNSHINE SPARKLES ON THE GOOD AND ON THE EVIL!

Grayson had phoned the hospital while driving to tell them to expect Sandy. He pulled his jeep into the entrance driveway of the hospital emergency room. Quickly but gently, Grayson picked up Sandy and ran inside. A guard tried to tell him he could not leave his vehicle parked there, but Grayson ignored his order to stop and kept going.

"The keys are in it," Grayson shouted as he ran.

The hospital was hectic. Medics and nurses hurried in every direction.

"Help!" Grayson called.

Two nurses ran to him. They could see the blood on Sandy and that she was still unconscious. One of the nurses motioned for a gurney. It was there within seconds. Grayson placed Sandy on the movable bed.

The E.R. doctor rushed over, took one look at Sandy's wounds and nodded to the nurses. "STAT!" he said. Then he hurried to talk to the surgeon.

The nurses went into overdrive, preparing Sandy for immediate surgery. Sandy had lost a lot of blood. They started an IV and took a blood sample to get the correct blood type for a transfusion if needed. Even though they had access to her employee records, they always ran the blood type to guarantee it was listed correctly. Grayson stayed right by her side. Two attendants rushed to Sandy and hurriedly pushed her toward the operating room for surgery.

"Wait here," one of the nurses told Grayson. "It's perfect you called ahead."

Grayson stood silently. He watched them wheel Sandy down the hall and through the double doors. Pausing, Grayson started praying. Suddenly, he stood erect and hurried out of the hospital emergency room entrance.

He ran as fast as he could. Grayson found his jeep parked in a space close to the entrance. He grabbed a shirt from his gym bag in the back seat, put it on, and got behind the wheel. Frantically, Grayson slammed the door shut and drove like a maniac out of the hospital parking lot.

***

James was in his office, and the secure phone rang. He answered. "Sergeant Richards." He grabbed a pad and pen and started writing as fast as possible. "Stop all outbound commercial and charter flights. Immediate arrest for Manuel Martinez. Got it, Grayson," he said.

***

Manuel slammed his car trunk shut and ran into the hotel. He was driven and furious. He was angry enough to kill quickly and looked for someone to hurt. He felt it was bad enough to be tricked, but to be deceived by a female to him was even worse.

***

Carol and Mark rushed into the hospital and down the hall. They went to the desk to request Sandy's room number, but she was still in surgery. The receptionist directed them to sit down in the waiting area.

"What could have happened?" Mark asked Carol, his voice filled with frustration. "Why would Sandy be in surgery? And why won't you tell me what's going on?"

"Most of it, I don't know," Carol admitted. "And of what I do know, I don't know what I can say. So, we just have to wait. And if truth be told, I'm not as patient as many people think I am."

Mark was stunned. Frantically, Carol put her hands on her face and took deep breaths. She closed her eyes and then abruptly turned to Mark. "Do you pray?" she asked.

Mark was silent. Then he responded, "No. Not really."

Carol took Mark's hands. "Well, now's a good time to start."

***

Rapidly leaving his hotel room, Manuel rushed down the hall carrying items to his car and putting them into the trunk. He then stepped in behind the wheel and sat down. "What do they know?" he growled, slamming the door. He pulled out of the parking lot and headed into the night. Manuel drove feverishly closer to the dunes and attempted to park more discretely. Grabbing tools, he hurried to the dunes.

***

After what seemed like forever to Carol and Mark, a doctor came into the waiting area wearing surgical scrubs. He walked over to Carol and Mark to talk to them. At first, he stood as he spoke. "Your friend survived. Quite honestly, she's lucky to be alive."

The doctor pulled up a chair, sat down, and continued. "She has lost a lot of blood from a knife stab to her spleen and had to be transfused. She has a punctured lung, broken ribs, and a repaired spleen and throat. At one point, we thought we would need to remove her spleen, but we were able to repair it. All that considered, it isn't nearly as bad as it could have been. She's in recovery in section three. One of you can go in with her in a few minutes. It's down that hall," he said, pointing the direction as he stood. "I wish your friend the best," he said and quickly left.

"What a relief. Sandy's alive," Carol said. "I wanted to ask the surgeon questions, but I was so stunned I couldn't even think. And me a nurse. Go figure. Oh, and I'm sorry I was so terse before, Mark. I was truly petrified. But that's no excuse."

"It's okay. I understand," Mark responded.

"Well, let's go see our girl," Carol smiled.

"They said only one of us can go in," Mark reminded Carol.

"What are they going to do, shoot us at sunrise?" Carol said, shrugging her shoulders.

Mark and Carol entered the Recovery Area with the sections partitioned off, each one having four beds. They discretely walked by the nurses' station and the first two sections, then came to section three. Of the four beds, only two were occupied, one by Sandy. They quietly entered and moved toward her. Carol was shaking and trying not to cry.

They saw that Sandy was bandaged and attached to various monitoring devices. She had an IV in her hand and a drainage tube coming from her lung. Carol and Mark tiptoed closer. Mark coughed, and the other patient groaned but kept sleeping.

Carol glared at Mark. "Sshhh." She looked at Sandy and gave in to her tears. Sandy slept soundly for another thirty minutes and then began to awaken.

Slowly, Sandy opened her eyes. She looked at Carol and spoke softly.

"Hi," Sandy said faintly.

"We didn't mean to wake you," Carol said.

Mark took Sandy's hand and smiled. "Glad you made it through surgery," Mark smiled.

"Me, too—"

Carol stopped Sandy. "Don't talk. You've got to heal."

Sandy insistently talked with difficulty. "Please, listen to me."

"What is it? I'm listening," Carol replied.

"Locate Grayson," Sandy whispered desperately. "He thinks he knows everything. But he doesn't. Manuel has something attached to his back. I think he's a human bomb!"

"Oh, no. We'll find Grayson," Carol promised.

"Who's Manuel?" Mark asked.

***

Grayson kicked open Manuel's hotel room door. He entered and searched the room, including under the bed, for Manuel. He checked the bathroom and then heard a noise.

An Arab hotel worker came to the door carrying a crate. "Is Mr. Sorrell here?" he asked.

"No," Grayson responded. He was surprised the hotel worker did not even look at the lock area, although there was not much to see unless you knew where to look.

The hotel worker placed the crate inside the door. "I'll leave this for him. He always tells me to place it in here."

"Always?" Grayson asked. "He gets these often?"

"Oh, yes. Please tell Mr. Sorrell I will be by tomorrow for his leftovers. We all love them, especially the soldiers," the worker replied.

"Thank you," Grayson said curiously.

After the hotel worker left, Grayson looked at the crate and closed the door. He opened the container and was puzzled by the contents. He picked up one of the packages and looked at it.

Caramel Popcorn Ball was printed on the label. Grayson ripped several popcorn balls apart but found nothing. He searched deeper into the pile, tossing popcorn balls on the floor. He took one from the middle. It said *Plain Popcorn Ball* on the label.

Grayson ripped the popcorn ball apart. Inside there was a packet of explosives. He opened more plain popcorn balls, finding receivers in some and explosives in others. He put them in separate piles, took out his secure phone, and called.

"James, the items, receivers, and explosives are coming inside popcorn balls. Hotel delivery. Devious plan but brilliant." Grayson hung up.

His phone rang, and he answered it. "Grayson." He listened intently. It was Carol. "Sandy's okay? She's going to be fine? That's great news," Grayson said.

Carol explained what Sandy had told her regarding Manuel. "What?" He became quiet. "Got it—human bomb. Thanks. Please take care of Sandy." He paused. "And yourself."

***

Nurse Ann Holland entered Sandy's section. Mark scurried over to the other patient's bed. Mark's quick thinking bought them a little time. The nurse tended to Sandy, checking all of her tubes, pumps, and monitors. She changed out Sandy's IV bag.

"Your color is looking good. Being a nurse, too, I know you understand all this. What is your pain level, and how are you feeling?" Nurse Holland asked Sandy.

"I hurt. Right now, about an eight," Sandy replied.

"We'll up your pain meds some. As you know, pain makes you tense up, which worsens the pain, and we don't want that." Nurse Holland injected medication into Sandy's IV line.

Then Holland moved to the other sleeping patient in the room, Mrs. Bentley. Mark put his pointer finger to his lips in a shushing motion and smiled toward Carol. Nurse Holland just checked the IV line, smiled at Mark, and left.

Later, Mrs. Bentley's husband tried to get in the room to see her, but the nursing staff thought she already had a visitor, Mark.

When Mr. Bentley complained and exposed Mark's deception, both Mark and Carol got in trouble for visiting with Sandy at the same time. Now, they were regularly being watched and had to take turns.

Sandy was waking up and falling back asleep. She recovered fairly rapidly from her anesthesia. It helped that whenever she woke up again, she would see either Carol or Mark. When fully awake and not dizzy, she was able to leave the recovery section with primary IV pain medication and all her attachments.

Sandy was glad to be out of the place where all the walls were just curtains, and every sound could be heard throughout the entire area. Happily, Sandy moved into a private room.

The nurse ensured Sandy's connections and her lung tube were working correctly for monitoring. "Your friends will be in very soon," the nurse reassured Sandy as she left.

Sergeant Brown, from the base gate, walked up to the door. He had initially met Sandy when she brought the chocolate chip cookies while looking for Grayson's identity. He knocked on her door frame. Sandy smiled, and he walked over to her bedside.

"Those were great cookies, ma'am. When do you think we can get some more?" he asked.

Sandy laughed and struggled with pain. "Soon, I hope."

Brown smiled. "When we met, you were looking for a hero. And from what I've heard through the grapevine, you've become one." He chuckled and nodded his head.

"That's a powerful word. I think I'd rather just be nursing the real heroes," she responded with a huge smile.

Sergeant Brown patted her arm. "If you need anything, I'll be on guard duty at your door. Lt. Colonel Grayson's orders, ma'am." Sergeant Brown headed back toward the door.

"Hey," Sandy said. "Does your grapevine tell you why Lt. Colonel Grayson doesn't have a girlfriend or a wife? Did he have a fiancée who died?"

Brown walked back to Sandy's bed. "Wish she had," he responded in a whisper. "If it had been me, she would've," he stated emphatically.

"What?" Sandy asked in surprise.

"You didn't hear this from me, but years ago, his fiancée ran off with his own brother! Can you believe that?" he sincerely questioned. "His own brother. So, he lost his fiancée and his brother."

"That's awful!" Sandy said.

"Yeah. It made him swear off women. But don't mention it. It's still a touchy subject," Brown admitted.

Carol and Mark entered the room. "Doc says you'll be in here a while," Carol reported.

"They must watch everything, mostly the tube to your punctured lung and your repaired spleen. Those will take the longest time to heal of all your injuries," Mark said.

"Your surgeon told us when we first met him, right after your surgery, that you are lucky to be alive," Carol added.

"We're all lucky you're alive," Mark confessed and took Sandy's hand.

A nurse entered and began scolding the visitors. "Only one at a time in here. Those doctor's orders are still in effect for now. And all you visitors know that." The nurse scowled at each of them.

***

Grayson left the hotel wildly and entered his jeep. As he was driving, he spotted Manuel's car parked in the furthermost area of the parking lot. He raced back into the hotel, feverishly looking for Manuel once again. Grayson knew Manuel was trying to hide his car. He immediately called Ortega to bring a special team, including snipers, to the hotel.

***

Brown had moved to his guard position outside Sandy's door. Carol insisted Mark stay with Sandy. She thought they looked so sweet, with Mark holding Sandy's hand. "I'll be back shortly. I'll get us some food and sneak back in when they're busy," Carol chuckled.

"And you a nurse," Mark laughed.

***

Ortega had the hotel surrounded and Manuel's car guarded from a safe distance. They wanted to catch him alive without alerting him. They needed his information.

Grayson exited the hotel again with several guys who came with Ortega. "He's not in there. He must be at the dunes," Grayson said and started running toward the sand.

Ortega and four soldiers followed Grayson. Other soldiers were surrounding the hotel and grounds. As they approached the dunes, Grayson saw sand flying erratically. He knew that had to be Manuel frantically digging.

Manuel was at the dunes. He was digging like a madman but finding nothing. Grayson appeared, gun drawn, at the top of the dune.

"Lose something?" Grayson shouted.

Manuel jumped up and grabbed a cord from his shirt. He was furious. "Stop! Suicide cord. I'll blow up both of us and half this country," he shouted.

"You may get us from your vest explosives. But currently, all signals are being jammed so the bombs will not explode. That's all you'll get, you and me." Grayson declared.

Ortega had circled around the dune and appeared behind Manuel with his gun aimed. He had the guys stay back in case Manuel came toward the car or hotel. Also, in case there was an explosion.

Manuel was focused entirely on Grayson. "We'll see. But first, I want you to hear how much I enjoyed feeding your soldiers my packing material. They loved the caramel popcorn balls. The irony was—"

Ortega could see that Manuel's finger was currently not on the trigger, just the cord. "Pack this," Ortega shouted and shot the back of Manuel's hand holding the rope. Manuel immediately let go of the cable and grabbed his hand.

"Nice shot," Grayson shouted.

Manuel hysterically searched for the cord with his other hand. Grayson jumped on Manuel to keep him from getting the cable again. They struggled as Ortega watched. Grayson landed strong blows, but Manuel, a World Class Martial Arts expert, managed to pull off some impressive kicks and punches. Manuel fought with only one hand, but it was a surprisingly fierce battle. Both men landed blows. Finally, Grayson got Manuel pinned to the ground and subdued him.

"This is not your day to die," Grayson declared.

Several GIs gathered on the dune with Ortega. They watched intently. Grayson zip-tied Manuel's wrists behind his back. He pulled open Manuel's shirt, revealing a bomber's vest.

Grayson examined the contents, front and rear. He pulled out folded pages, looked at them, and then at Ortega.

"No explosives. Just maps. Fake person. A fake suicide bomber," Grayson said. He motioned for the soldiers to come down the dune to get Manuel.

"Take him. Tend to his hand," Ortega called.

Grayson unfolded the papers and studied them intently. Ortega joined him, and Grayson handed some map pages to Ortega. One of the GIs bandaged Manuel's hand.

"Maps of burial sites of the explosives and receivers, with quantity lists. It does have to be accurate to work," Grayson said.

"These are maps of the palace and the royal family's treasure room," Ortega pointed to the area on his paper.

"Ah, now we know why Manuel is here—for the valuables. He never does anything out of principle, only greed. It looks like we hit the jackpot with these maps."

Manuel snarled. "No. The jackpot is the explosions and kidnappings that will be happening all over the globe. People will be dying and suffering, and you can't stop it."

Grayson looked at Ortega, then at Manuel.

"But we have you," Ortega said with a smirk.

"I know my rights. You'll never get me to talk," Manuel insisted.

"Maybe not. But I bet the Saudis will," Grayson replied.

"Hence, we don't need you," Ortega added.

"So, do it. Just go ahead, shoot me," Manuel ordered.

"Shooting's too good for you," Grayson responded.

Ortega stared at Manuel. "We're turning you over to the Saudis. Relax. You're the assassin here. We're not going to kill you," Ortega said.

Grayson winked at Ortega. "Although, you may wish we had by the time the Saudis are finished with you, especially going after one of their princesses. They are very protective of the royal family members. Yep. You are going to suffer a very long, hard stretch," Grayson warned Manuel with a smirk.

Five more GIs came over the dune. One of them looked sternly at Manuel. "Hey, you're Carson's friend," he yelled.

Ortega was shocked and became enraged. He turned red and went after Manuel. Ortega slammed him back against the dune with his hands.

"My men! So, you and Carson are behind the sand problems and helicopter and aircraft explosions!" Ortega said through gritted teeth.

Ortega picked up Manuel by his shirt. "You're not the only one who'll be wishin' he was dead." Ortega got angrier with every syllable. "Maybe—"

Grayson pulled Ortega off Manuel. "It's not worth getting in trouble. He's not worth it. We need you free to fight all the bad guys," Grayson said.

Ortega fought his emotions. He loved his men and felt responsible for them, somewhat like a father. Getting a grip on his anger, he calmed down.

Grayson pointed to the soldiers. "You two, take him to the holding cell," he instructed.

Manuel fought his captors every step. He struggled with all his might but was no match for them.

Grayson patted the shoulder of the GI who recognized Manuel as Carson's friend. "Looks like you just won Project Sand Dollar. Which charity are you going for?" Grayson asked.

"Sir, I want all the money divided among the families of our fallen heroes. Even my share," he replied.

Ortega was now calm. "Nice choice, son," Ortega said. He turned to Grayson. "See what great guys these are." Ortega smiled.

"Absolutely," Grayson responded. "A few bad apples won't spoil the whole bunch if you catch them in time. Not with honorable characters like this guy. We just have to weed out the rotten ones."

"How did this even happen?" Ortega asked adamantly.

Grayson shook his head. "It seems like some rotten ones are in the higher ranks lately. Like you said, 'Selling their souls and selling out the country all for a buck.' We need to do some house cleaning and fast!"

Chapter Sixteen

STARTING ANEW

Medic Collins entered the GI hospital ward where various wounded soldiers were hooked up to IVs. Medic Collins walked over to the corner bed with something in his hand.

"I told you you'd make it. Here," Medic Collins said, handing Hoffman the photo of his kids. "I had the photo scanned and cleaned. You can take care of your kids yourself."

Tears flooded Hoffman's eyes as he touched the picture and smiled. "Thank you," he said, full of gratitude for Collins and for being alive.

Medic Collins pulled the old, bloody photo from his pocket. "Oh, and here. Keep this one, so you'll know how lucky you are."

Hoffman looked at the bloody photograph. "Right now, I sure feel very thankful," he said as tears once again filled his eyes. "Coming so close to death will get your mind real straight. And fast! All the little things that seemed so important turn out to be just that—little things that don't matter. What a waste of time and energy. Since I will be okay, it was worth getting hurt just to learn that valuable lesson."

***

The sun was still shining outside the aircraft hangar. Arseneault was on a tall ladder wiping down a plane. Two MPs entered the hangar.

"We're here to get Carson. You did detain him, right?" the taller MP asked.

Arseneault put his stuff down and hopped off the ladder. "Yeah. He's back here," Arseneault replied and led the way.

The MPs followed Arseneault to the back corner of the hangar. Carson's hands and feet were zip-tied. He had been severely beaten. Surprised, the MPs looked at each other.

"He had kind of a ladder accident," Arseneault explained.

Arseneault looked at Carson. Carson's eyes were almost swollen shut. Carson looked at Arseneault and then at the MPs. He spoke through swollen lips.

"That's right. What Arseneault said," Carson sheepishly responded.

Arseneault went back to his plane. The MPs took Carson and looked at each other repeatedly. Just before exiting the hangar, they stopped. The taller and more senior MP called, "Hey, Arseneault." He stopped what he was doing and looked their way. Both MPs smiled and simultaneously each gave Arseneault a thumbs-up. Then they nodded as they took Carson out of the hangar.

***

Grayson arrived at Ortega's tent in his jeep. Ortega walked out to meet him.

"You were right," Ortega said. "Manuel's singing like a bird and spilling his guts on everything. He's petrified of being turned over to the Saudis. Great idea." Ortega chuckled.

"What about those satellite dish enhancement boxes?" Grayson asked.

"Those boxes have repeaters that help transmit the signals to the explosives. We're jamming all the signals until we retrieve every last explosive," Ortega reported.

"Fantastic," Grayson smiled.

"Manuel's spilling the beans on everyone," Ortega continued. "Carson and four other guys who had access to the military and police aircraft were creating the sand problems. Some of them will be facing murder charges. And it was all for money. Not one religious zealot in the lot. This whole plan is way bigger than it seems. They're still working on the big picture. We're lucky it got stopped. It's a good day."

"It sure is," Grayson replied emphatically. He was very thankful Sandy and the real Drockden were alive. Once again, Grayson was re-examining his whole existence. He had been thinking hard about every aspect of everything and everyone in his life.

***

Sandy lay in her hospital bed while Mark sat in the chair beside her, holding her hand. He had not left her side except to go to the bathroom. Carol hurried down the hall and entered Sandy's room. She sat in the chair on the other side of the bed.

"They got Drockden! Manuel, that is. And Grayson is fine," Carol said gleefully. "He's on his way here."

"Oh, thank goodness. What an absolute nightmare," Sandy responded.

"Yeah," Mark said with his eyes wide. "I can't believe you two were involved in all this. It's unreal."

Grayson walked into the room. "How are you doing?" he asked Sandy.

"Super. I'm so glad you caught Manuel. He is majorly creepy. That makes everything worth it," Sandy replied.

"I'm very thankful, too. Had Manuel succeeded, those plans would have been devastating," Grayson responded. "And I'm thrilled you're okay. We all owe you a powerful debt of gratitude! I'm working on getting you some recognition."

Carol gave a big grin. "The Saudis want Manuel. I wonder what his punishment will be?"

Grayson laughed and shook his head. "Manuel and his criminal partners planned to abduct the princess and steal the entire fortune from the treasure room during the confusion of the explosions. That's a lot of treasure—jewels, gold, and more. For them, it was all about the money. They would be wealthy and make their boss happy by getting him the princess he has wanted for so long. With all the confusion, it would take a while to realize Zahwah was even missing. And with the explosions and carnage, everyone would blame extremists and never think to look in Mexico."

"Is that why they kept messing with the aircraft?" Carol asked. "To blame the extremists?"

"Yes, exactly," Grayson replied. "But getting caught is really serious. The Saudis are very protective of their princesses. And their treasuries. And their country."

Sandy yawned. "What about the explosives he stuffed in the sand? That's scary."

Grayson nodded in agreement. "They're all being collected right now. Thanks to you," Grayson paused and smiled at Sandy. "We found detailed maps of where every buried explosive and repeater is. Manuel's group is filling in the rest. They're telling it all. What a plan," Grayson said.

Mark sighed. "So, actually, Drockden, I mean Manuel's sand trap was foiled by the Sandy trap," Mark said.

They all groaned and then laughed. Mark kissed Sandy's hand.

"Ugh. That was bad. But good too." Carol smiled.

Mark lovingly looked at Sandy. "What a way to go, though. I may be caught in a Sandy trap myself," Mark admitted.

Carol winced and rolled her eyes as the nurse entered. They had been caught again, breaking the visitor rule.

"Still only one at a time. Out. Now. I'll be back in three minutes," the nurse said.

"Sorry. See you later, Sandy," Carol said as she rose to go.

"Yeah, see ya later, kid," Grayson said. Closer to the door, he beat Carol out of the room, then paused to talk with Sergeant Brown.

As Carol neared the door, Sandy looked intently at her. "Carol, you're not done," Sandy said.

"What do you need?" Carol asked, turning back.

Sandy looked even more intently at Carol and then turned to Mark. "Can you please give us a minute?" she asked. "Girl talk."

"Sure," Mark replied. He walked out of the room as Carol moved closer to Sandy.

"You're not done. Maybe you should bake some cookies for Grayson," Sandy advised.

Carol grasped the message. Her eyes widened, and she gave a grimacing look toward Sandy.

"Could you fluff my pillow, please?" Sandy asked.

Carol came closer and fluffed the pillow. Mark was thumbing through magazines in the hall.

"Be nice to Grayson. His fiancée ran off with his brother. His own brother! So, there's no dead love to haunt you," Sandy said with a huge grin.

"Interesting but irrelevant," Carol replied.

Sandy whispered to Carol, "No live one either; I've got my guy." Sandy smiled and pointed toward Mark.

Carol chuckled and gave Sandy a thumbs-up of approval. "Oh, I'm so glad. Mark is crazy about you. But I'm still done."

Sandy patted Carol's arm. "And people think I'm the dumb one," Sandy responded, tilting her head to the side.

Carol shook her head and walked to the door. "Get well. Love ya," she said and waved. "I'll be back later."

***

Sergeant Brown felt guilty and had admitted to Grayson that he had told Sandy about Grayson's brother and fiancée. Brown was concerned that Grayson might find out and thought it would be better if he confessed. Brown was surprised that Grayson took the news so well. They were still talking as Carol walked out of the room.

"Thanks," Grayson said to Sergeant Brown.

"Thank you, sir," he replied.

Carol turned back and waved. "Bye," she said.

"Goodbye, ma'am," the guard said.

Carol walked down the hall. Sergeant Brown and Grayson exchanged salutes, and Grayson hurried after Carol.

"Hey, come with me," Grayson said as he reached Carol.

"Uh, okay," she responded, somewhat caught off guard.

Grayson took Carol by the hand. They hurried down the hall and into an empty stairwell area.

"Let's celebrate," he said.

"Huh?" Carol was confused.

Still holding Carol's hand, Grayson embraced Carol and kissed her passionately. When they finally stopped, Carol opened her eyes slowly.

"It wasn't just the moment," she said, with her eyes half closed.

"What?" he asked.

"Never mind," she whispered as her heart pounded.

Grayson looked into Carol's eyes and stroked her cheek.

"Something's happened," he said softly. "I don't know what caused it—the thing with Drockden, almost losing Sandy, or finding you. But I've realized ..." Grayson paused and kissed Carol again, even longer and more fervently. He smiled at her and ran his fingers through her hair.

"Life's too short and can be too wonderful to let the past steal today or tomorrow," he admitted enthusiastically. "I want us to get married and have a family and a magnificent life. I want to let go of the past and hold onto you forever!"

Carol looked intently at Grayson and smiled. "I guess I'm not done."

Grayson looked deeply into Carol's eyes, and she could barely breathe. He smiled. "You know, you have made any residual resentment I had toward my brother and my ex-fiancée disappear. It's gone. All I feel is more joy and love than I ever had. I am so glad they're together. So, I can be with you. Oh, and I feel tremendous gratitude and love for you! You are incredible, and I am very blessed and so much in love with you. We may even invite my brother and ex to the wedding. God does work in wonderous ways."

"When we let Him," Carol added, smiling and nodding her head. I've had some issues myself. But none of it seems to matter now. I love you, too. I didn't want to admit it, but I do. Very much. God is amazing."

"Maybe love conquers pain?" Grayson said.

"Well, right now, it sure feels like love heals it," Carol admitted and smiled. "So, since we're getting married, what is your first name?"

Grayson got a funny look and said, "Well, my grandmother and mother were both huge Cary Grant fans. They always thought he was so genuine and delightful."

Carol smiled. "Cary Grayson. I like it."

Rubbing his chin, Grayson grimaced. "Ah, not even close. It's Archibald, Cary Grant's real name."

Carol started laughing and so did Grayson. "So, Grayson it is. I love that name," Carol said.

"Me, too," Grayson added with a charming nod and a chuckle.

They passionately kissed for a very long time, creating the start of a beautiful story they will share with their children and grandchildren.

Happily-ever-afters are real!

FORTUNATELY, NOT THE END

Epilogue Follows

Epilogue

Sam was seated at his expensive African Blackwood desk in his opulent office. He was very old and somewhat haggard. The butler served him a red beverage. He drank some, and the phone rang. He answered it and listened.

"Yeah. So, they got Drockden's look-alike. So, what? That's just one down. We still have twelve major areas operational."

Sam counted with his fingers as he spoke. "Rome, Chicago, London, and New York have checked in. I'm waiting to hear from the others."

The butler straightened the couch pillows as Sam continued.

"Tell me, did they buy the bit about the Mexican drug cartel?"

Sam smiled, hung up the phone, and finished his drink. The butler started to pick up the glass.

"Oh, sir. You received an odd telephone message. I wrote it down," the butler said.

"READ IT." Sam snapped in his typical ugly manner.

The butler took a paper from his pocket, opened it, and began. "'It's tragic you spent so much time with your sadistic, torturous, Nazi grandfather growing up. The things you endured were horrible.'"

Sam slammed down his glass. "Who was this?" he demanded.

"A voice on the secure phone, sir," the butler answered.

Sam was livid. "My computer hacks will find him. Continue!"

The butler looked at the paper. "'However, no matter how much someone is hurt, it's no excuse to hurt others like the beaten boy or girl who grows up and hits his or her children. It's wrong. He or she is wrong. It's evil.'"

Sam threw his empty glass; it landed unbroken across the room.

"Should I continue, sir? There's more," the butler asked.

"Read!" Sam barked.

The butler continued. "'You've spent your life claiming to be an atheist. But the majority of atheists have some morals and integrity. Not you. You even give atheists a bad name.

"'Many people do not know that Hitler, especially his elite SS, had ties to and rituals for Satan. They even had Satanic gold rings made with a skull-type head for each member of the exclusive SS. The rings supposedly offered power that came from the dark forces. Your grandfather was a member of the SS when he was only fourteen. And I see that you proudly wear his occult ring. Perhaps that's the difference between you and your brother. You have pursued your grandfather's footsteps in following Satan and evil. So, you know very well that God is real. Your supposed atheism is just a ruse. You simply prefer evil over good. Hurting people pleases you. But you have never comprehended that Satan is not loyal to his followers. Like all the others, *you have been manipulated and used*. He just wanted your soul, and he's got it. There are *Happy Endings*, but not for you. You chose evil. You enjoyed evil. You are doomed, or more appropriately, damned.' That was it, sir."

Sam was furious and slamming things everywhere. The butler started to leave but turned back.

"Oh. You have another message from a different person." The butler got out another piece of paper from a different pocket.

"The others will not be checking in. By now, Rome, Chicago, London, and New York are shut down. We have lists of all your plans and your people. You lose."

Sam was outraged. He picked up the phone and pushed a button. "Track every call received today. Now!" Sam slammed down the phone.

The butler looked at his watch, then placed the second unfolded piece of paper on Sam's desk. It was blank.

"That last message was from me. This time, the butler did do it. You should not have killed all those people, many of them innocent. And hurt so many more. By the International Justice Alliance, you have been found guilty of countless murders and atrocities and of hurting innumerable countries and people."

"I've never even heard of the International Justice Alliance!" Sam shouted furiously.

"Most people haven't. You are not the only one working behind the scenes. Except, we work for the good of humankind, not evil." The butler smiled and pointed at Sam.

"You have committed many crimes against humanity. It must stop. And we could only conceive of one way to end the murder of innocents. Hope you liked your drink."

Sam was in shock and confused. He stared at the butler.

The butler stared back. "Now, I don't buy the poor little boy routine. Your brother had the same awful childhood you did. The same torture, the same pain, the same cruelty, and he's a fine, good man. You are evil because you choose to be. Being evil, like being good, is a *choice*. Each of us makes our own choice. Unfortunately, you made the wrong one, and many people suffered." The butler looked at his watch.

He continued. "Oh, we also hope that when people realize that many of your big companies knowingly make lots of obscene profits by using slave labor in countries such as China or Africa, the public will no longer buy those products. No matter how many gimmicks or celebrities are employed. Most people are ultimately good and do not want to be part of or responsible for causing or contributing to slavery or misery. Anywhere! *Especially against children!*"

"But...but...who are you?" Sam asked.

"Right now, I'm the timekeeper, and you've got about two minutes. Countless people will live because we finally uncovered your plans and all those involved in them."

Sam panicked. He gasped and began to choke as the butler picked up the papers from the desk and polished the wood. Then, the butler retrieved the glass from across the room and put it in his pocket. Exiting the office, he left with a parting thought.

"Like it or not, our choices eventually do have consequences. Totally up to us whether they are good or bad. That's why it's important to choose our actions wisely. Right decisions equal fewer regrets. You blew it!" the butler said as he wiped off both sides of the entrance knob and closed the door with finality and finesse.

The butler thought as he quietly entered the night, *One murderous monster down. Many more to go...*

"Put on the whole armour of God, that ye may be able to stand against the wiles of the devil. For we wrestle not against flesh and blood, but against principalities, against powers, against the rulers of the darkness of this world, against spiritual wickedness in high places."

The New Testament, Ephesians 6:11&12 (King James Version)

"Those who expect to reap the blessing of freedom
must undertake to support it."
—THOMAS PAINE

"The price of freedom is eternal vigilance."
THOMAS JEFFERSON